For More Visit:

THE YOUNG WRITERS SOCIETY

http://www.YoungWritersSociety.com

THE YOUNG WRITERS LITERARY JOURNAL VOLUME II

Edited by Nathaniel Lee Caldwell

Edited by Omar Sakr

Cover Art by Adam Singletary

YOUNG WRITERS SOCIETY PUBLISHERS

Bethesda

Young Writers Society Publishers

Bethesda, MD

www.YoungWritersSociety.com

ISBN: 978-0-578-05369-1

First Edition: March 2010

Printed in the United States of America

TABLE OF CONTENTS

COPYRIGHT AND ACKNOWLEDGEMENTS

All of the works are copyright in the name of their individual authors. Because many authors are below the age of 18, their surnames have been abbreviated.

"101 Tips for Writers" © 2007 by Nathaniel L. Caldwell. First Publication, original to this anthology. Printed by permission of the author.

"About Something" © 2009 by Siiri T. First Publication, original to this anthology. Printed by permission of the author.

"Assistance in Endings" © by Matthew D. First Publication, original to this anthology. Printed by permission of the author.

"Autumn Kissed" © by Sophie W. First Publication, original to this anthology. Printed by permission of the author.

"Azaleas for Susie" © by Kelley D. First Publication, original to this anthology. Printed by permission of the author.

"Branding" © by Kristin O. First Publication, original to this anthology. Printed by permission of the author.

"Burnt Sausages" © by Mark C. First Publication, original to this anthology. Printed by permission of the author.

"Christmas Magic" © by Alexa O. First Publication, original to this anthology. Printed by permission of the author.

"Chromatography" © by Baqiyyah H. First Publication, original to this anthology. Printed by permission of the author.

"Dog" © Photo by Michelle K. First Publication, original to this anthology. Printed by permission of the author.

"Evergreen" © by Kylan R. First Publication, original to this anthology. Printed by permission of the author.

"First Kiss" © by Cassaundra E. First Publication, original to this anthology. Printed by permission of the author.

PREFACE

Omar Sakr

Hundreds of countries; thousands of states; billions of people; millions of teenagers; a multitude of cultures connected by one element: the power of story. Story has been one of the defining threads of society since the beginning of time – since the cavemen painted upon crude walls basic images and simple recounts, humanity has distinguished itself from and elevated itself above, the animal kingdom, through the power of thought and imagination. It's through the power of story that the world as we know it has been defined; with it, mystics and priests devised complex mythologies and pantheons of gods to explain away the night and day, the seasons of weather; natural disasters; diseases and all other manner of unknowable wonders that have become common knowledge today.

Throughout history, we have evidence of certain stories – of people and philosophies – that have wrought massive change upon reality as we know it. The stories of Prince Siddhartha, Abraham, Moses, Jesus and Muhammad have inspired millions for a thousand years and on, impacting on society (in most of these cases) so much so that our very nature and way of living was altered in the aftermath. More recently, the modern day lives of Mahatma Ghandi, Martin Luther King, John. F. Kennedy, Yasser Arafat, Adolf Hitler, Stalin, Bush and Bin Laden along with many more have changed not only the face of history but the climate in which we live. From political rhetoric to gossip magazines, from the dominance of the novel to the rise of radio and cinematic masterpieces, society has been spun from the stuff of narratives both personal and national, real and imagined.

Today, we are inundated with an unprecedented level and variety of stories. The mass media – newspapers, news programs, magazines, radio and the internet – bombards us with such a confusing morass that it can be hard to find a place to stand tall, to distinguish yourself, and have your voice heard. Given the long standing arrogance and prejudice with which teenagers and young adults have been regarded by both society at large and the publishing world, having your voice heard with any seriousness is a difficult task indeed.

Since its inception in 2004, the Young Writers Society has strived to create just such a space and through its emphasis on friendly encouragement and improvement; its adherence to proper guidelines and the ideals of free speech without censorship and most importantly, its fostering of community spirit, it has done just that and with an ever-increasing membership of more than 9, 000, it has proved to be a successful formula.

It's not always easy to do. In fact, sometimes it's downright painful and disheartening, with the pressure to succeed, the realities of the publishing market and plethora of negative commentary beating down on already hunched backs but whatever the reason, we are bound by the singular drive to tell stories; to free our imaginations, ourselves and our readers on a whirlwind ride to elsewhere. Whether its to express long repressed emotions or to explore cultural spaces and haunted places, to uncover some elusive truth behind the contrivances of modernity and push boundaries or just simply to entertain, we need to write and so we do. The road is long and the process ongoing – it'll never end so long as your feet keep moving, no matter the path you're on, so don't hesitate, just walk. One day, you'll come to the end of the road and realise that the only footprints stretching back are your own, that there was no need to worry, to stress, or force yourself to hurry, you competed against yourself only.

Here now, we have brought together a collection of tales celebrating, unashamedly, our passion to tell stories for whatever reason we wish and I hope you find them as entertaining as I did. Each story is indicative of a different young writer, at a different stage in their journey. We tried to fid a place for each bracket and every voice that needed to be heard. Without further ado, please enjoy.

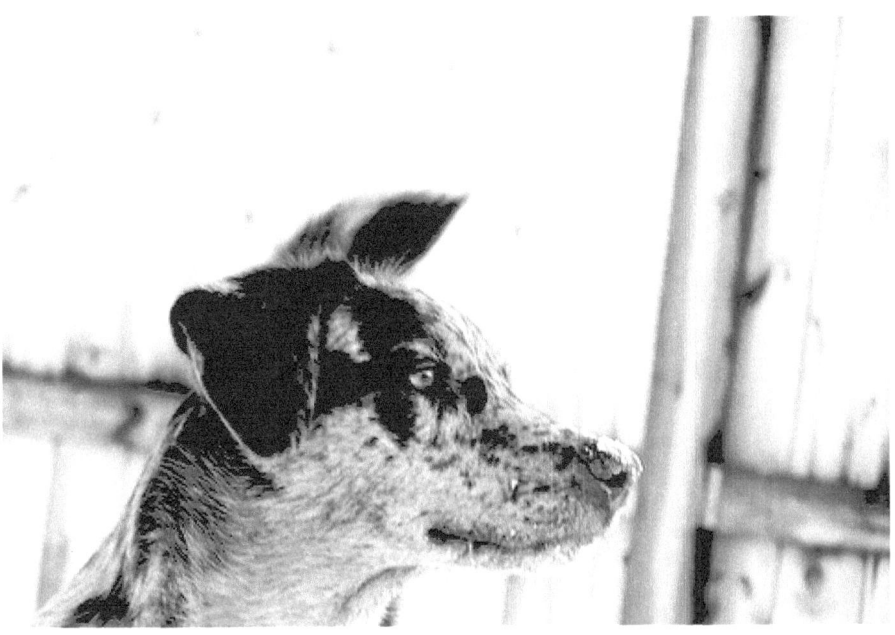

"Dog," a photo by Michelle K.; 17 (F) of British Columbia, Canada

101 TIPS FOR WRITERS

Nathaniel Lee Caldwell

The time to begin writing an article is when you have finished it to your satisfaction. By that time you begin to clearly and logically perceive what it is you really want to say.
-   Mark Twain

Whether you call yourself a young writer, a teenage writer, or just a writer, these tips are guidelines we should all follow. They apply not just to stories, but also to writing in general.

For your convenience, I have separated the 101 Tips for Writers into fifteen general topics: Set Up, Brainstorming, Pre-Writing, Beginning, While Writing, Descriptions, Characters, Dialogue, Grammar & Word Choice, Ending, Editing Process, The Review Process, The Post-Review Process, Beating Writer's Block, and General Tips. So go forth, read, and good luck!

Set Up

1. **Choose A Place:** Identify your best writing spot. Could be your room, the basement, the living room, the dog house, or, if you're really poetic, by a glistening stream.

2. **Organize:** Organize and clean your writing spot. An uncluttered room lends itself to an uncluttered mind.

3.   **Good Lighting:** Soft light? Bright light? No light? Sunlight? Lighting does make a difference, and you need to figure out which works best for you.

4.   **Temperature:** Pay attention to the temperature. Generally speaking, guys work best when the temperature is a bit colder than normal. Girls work best when the temperature is a bit warmer than normal.

5.   **Food:** Some people like to have something to nibble on when writing. Others don't. Figure out which group you belong to.

6.   **Noise:** If you prefer total silence then make sure you write somewhere silent. But if you like noise, play some music or TV.

7.   **Time:** Figure out what time of day you are in the writing zone. This will differ from person to person, and it may take a while before you figure out the perfect time of day for you.

Brainstorming

8.   **Keep A Journal:** Keeping a daily journal is the best way to keep your writing mind active.

9.   **Carry A Notepad:** Carry a notepad around with you to jot down ideas as they come to you.

10.   **Practice Writing Prompts:** Do a Google search for 'writing prompts.' Not only will these keep your writing mind engaged, but they are also a great source of ideas.

11.   **Relax:** Stress about brainstorming and your ideas will be no good. Best to relax and enjoy life. Ideas will come in good time.

12.   **Look Up Legal Cases:** Believe it or not, but legal cases are a great source of plots for stories. Go to http://www.findlaw.com/casecode and check a few.

13.   **Read:** Read, read, read! If you don't read, your mind will go to mush. If your mind goes to mush then you may as well write on napkins because that is all it will be good for.

14.   **Exercise:** You can keep your body active by just walking for thirty minutes. Keeping your body active will keep your mind active.

15.   **Study Other Writers:** When reading, don't just read, but analyze as well.

Pre-Writing

16.   **Write A Synopsis:** Write out a short one or two paragraph synopsis of the story before beginning anything else. A synopsis should be as general as possible.

17.   **Make Character Outlines:** List your main characters, and then add details even if you don't plan on using those details in the story.

18.   **Draw Scenes:** List the scenes in which your story will take place, then make simple drawings of them. Or, you can find photos of what you want your scene to look like.

19.   **Outline The Story:** Take your synopsis and add lots of detail to it. Outline in whatever fashion works for you.

20.   **Think It Over:** Before actually beginning, let the story sink into your mind for a few days.

21.   **Have Everything Ready:** Once you're almost ready to begin, make sure you have everything you need from carrots to paper.

Beginning

22.   **Do A Writing Prompt First:** You don't exercise without warming up, so why would you do differently when writing?

23.   **Relax, Let It Come:** Don't get worked up over the beginning. Your story will be the worse for it.

24.   **If In Trouble, Go For A Walk:** Walking will clear your mind.

25.   **Don't Edit, Just Write:** Push out the editor within yourself and just write. A first draft should be very rough, and you have plenty of time later to edit.

26.   **Turn On Some Background Noise:** Playing music, or just turning on something that makes noise like a fan, can help concentrate your mind on the task at hand.

27. **Start Off Generally:** Don't throw the reader into the middle of a plot. Get us introduced first.

28. **If In Trouble, Opt For A Classic Beginning:** Classic beginnings start with a description of what the character looks like, or a description of the scene. This can then build into the story.

While Writing

29. **Take Rest Breaks:** Even if you can, it is not a good idea to run a ten kilometer stretch all at once, and the same applies to writing. Take rest-breaks even when you are in the zone.

30. **Stay Awake And Alert:** If you find yourself getting tired or sleepy, stop!

31. **Don't Edit, Just Write:** Same as tip #21. If you are editing while writing, you will never complete your story.

32. **Know Your Unique Characteristics:** If you need food nearby, or if you can only write while swinging upside down from a water buffalo, know this and account for it.

Descriptions

33. **Draw Scenes:** Same as tip #18. Either drawing the scene (no matter how simplistic) or finding a photo of what you want the scene to look like will help you visualize the story.

34. **Make The Background Descriptive:** Be sure to describe the background. Doing so will draw the reader in.

35. **But Don't Over-Describe:** Just like a play only has general scenery, so should your story. Describing every plant, rock, and object will only bore your reader.

36. **Don't Use Too Many Adjectives:** Simply saying "the creaking door opened," is better than saying "the rust-ridden, brown, large rectangular door opened."

37. **Use Descriptive Verbs:** Saying "the wobbly bike" is better than saying "the bike looked like it was about to fall."

38. **Show, Don't Tell:** Saying "the wobbly bike" shows the reader that the bike is about to fall without overtly saying so.

Characters

39. **Love Your Characters, Even The Evil Ones:** If you truly love your characters, then adding depth comes naturally.

40. **Don't Be Too Cool:** No one likes a perfect character. Remember that flaws, especially of the fatal variety, are sexy.

41. **Base Your Characters On People You Know:** Basing a character on someone you know is a lot easier than making one up and you will end up with a much deeper story.

42. **Make Character Outlines:** Same as tip #17. It will be easier to explain your character's motives and histories if you outline everything about them.

43. **Give Your Character A History:** This person did not just pop out of nowhere. Give them a history showing us why we should care and why they are acting in such a manner.

44. **Ask Yourself Why:** Why is this character in the story? Why is she acting this way? Why should anyone care?

45. **How Do They Talk? Walk?:** The ways of talking and walking are unique to every person.

Dialogue

46. **Go To A Mall Or Park:** Just walking around or sitting in a very social setting will show you the different ways people talk.

47. **Listen:** Listen to what other people are saying around you and how they are talking.

48. **Have A Friend Read Out An Extended Conversation With You:** If you have a long conversation between two or more characters, then read it out loud with a group of people to make sure it makes sense and sounds right.

49.   **Nuances In Speaking:** Nobody speaks perfectly. In fact, far from it; each person has a unique way of talking.

50.   **Learn To Love Said:** Said is one of the few words a reader will automatically gloss over. Coming up with synonyms is at best unnecessary and at worse damaging to your story.

51.   **Use Quotation Marks:** Unless you are James Joyce, then use quotation marks. It does not matter if they are single or double; just be consistent.

52.   **Avoid Qualifying Said:** Be careful when you add a verb next to said, such as "quickly said" or "cautiously said." If you do your dialogue right, you won't need those extra verbs most of the time.

53.   **Know Who's Speaking:** With two characters, it is easy to tell who is speaking. But if you add more, make sure that the reader can follow who is speaking.

Grammar & Word Choice

54.   **Active Is Better Than Passive:** Using passive voice is weak and boring. Nobody says, "The theory that was formulated by Einstein." They say, "Einstein's theory."

55.   **Use Words People Know:** If you can show what the word means in the context, then good. But if you are sending your reader to the dictionary, then you are doing something wrong.

56.   **Don't Use Rarely Used Words:** There are certain rare words everyone knows, such as 'beseech' or 'arbor.' However, using a rare word will take your reader out of the story, so it is *usually* better to use common words.

57.   **Avoid Exclamation Marks:** Adding an exclamation mark is a cheap way to make something interesting and usually fails!

58.   **Avoid "Very":** Mark Twain once said, "Substitute 'damn' every time you're inclined to write 'very'; your editor will delete it and the writing will be just as it should be."

59.   **Always Toward, Never Towards. Its is not It's. Affect and Effect:** Know the differences between words, and know that words like 'towards' and 'alot' do not in fact exist.

60. **Use Spell Check, But Don't Rely On It:** Spell check is nice, but it want get al of you're miss steaks.

61. **Try To Avoid Split Infinitives:** Obviously, 'to boldly go' is better than 'to go boldly.' But if you can't make a case for using a split infinitive, then don't use it.

62. **Use A Thesaurus:** There are only a few words a reader will gloss over. Find synonyms for the others.

63. **Avoid That And This:** You should avoid that, and you should avoid this. 'That' and 'this' are not descriptive and have no place in stories.

64. ***Italics or Bold, But Not Both:*** Using italics or bold is a good way to emphasize words. But there is no need to do both.

65. **Commas At Natural Pauses:** Read, your sentence, aloud. If, a comma, makes you, stop, unnaturally then, remove, it.

66. **And Then... And Then... And Then:** If you find yourself saying 'and then' or even just 'then,' then your reader will become annoyed.

Ending

67. **Know Your Ending Before You Begin:** You shouldn't ever start a story without knowing how it will end.

68. **Stop Where The Story Ends:** Many writers want to keep writing even after the main story is over. Doing so just annoys the reader and makes the story drag on.

69. **Don't Leave The Reader Hanging... By Too Much:** Make sure you tie up all loose ends, but also make sure that you leave your reader wanting more.

70. **Leave It Alone For A While:** After you finish, leave the story alone for a few days.

Editing Process

71. **First, Revise:** After a few days pass, revision your story and ask yourself if that is how you wanted the story.

72.   **Second, Edit:** Brutalize your own work. Rework awkward sentences, ask yourself if that word is the right word, and make sure everything makes sense.

73.   **Third, Proofread:** When you proofread, you are checking your grammar. The best way to do this is to read it out loud. It can take a while, but you'll also catch a lot more miss steaks.

74.   **Show To Others:** Print out multiple copies of the story and pass it around to friends and family. They may not end up reading the whole thing, but they can still give you valuable insight.

75.   **Learn To Love The Drafting Process:** The first draft of Star Wars involved a guy named Kane Starkiller, a black knight, and Jedi Bendu. Thank God George Lucas didn't stop at a first draft.

The Review Process

76.   **Pass The Story Around:** Give your final copy to friends, family, and even literary magazines.

77.   **Put The Story Online:** Publishing your story online will give you instant access to people who actually want to read and review your work.

The Post-Review Process

78.   **Listen to Critiques:** When people critique your story, listen to them. You do not need to agree, but you should not argue either. They may be suggesting changes that would be worthwhile for you to consider.

79.   **Revisit Your Piece:** Even Star Wars isn't perfect, and George Lucas revisits it constantly. You should do the same with your story.

80.   **Makes Changes As Necessary:** If you really care about what you wrote, then you will correct mistakes and always seek to make the story better.

Beating Writer's Block

81.   **Take a Break:** If you have writer's block, then step away from your story rather than trying to force it.

82.   **Listen To Music:** Listening to music can help reduce stress.

83.   **Take a Shower:** Showering has a cleansing effect on the body and the mind.

84.   **Do Writing Prompts:** Find a few writing prompts, and do those.

85.   **Don't Think About The Story:** When you get writer's block, it is best to just go and do something else that does not involve thinking about the story. The way around the block will come to you when you least expect it.

General Tips

86.   **Practice:** In everything, practice makes perfect. Always write and never stop.

87.   **Read:** Reading cannot be emphasized enough. In fact, all of the tips on this list mean absolutely nothing if you do not read.

88.   **Pay Attention In School:** History will teach you how one event leads to another. Math will teach you how to think logically. English will teach you proper grammar.

89.   **Write With Emotion. Get Enthusiastic!:** You have to like what you are writing, and you have to be enthusiastic about it. Otherwise, why are you writing?

90.   **Never Give Up:** Writing is tough and grueling, but it is also rewarding.

91.   **Write For Yourself:** In the end, it only matters what you think.

92.   **Respect Editors:** If someone takes the time to read and review your work, then give them respect. You don't need to agree, but you don't need to tell them to shove it either.

93.   **Find Your Inspiration:** Find out what motivates you to write, and then use that to keep writing.

94.   **Take Your Time:** When writing a story, it's best to take it slow.

95.   **Have Confidence:** Be confident about what you write. Some people will like it and others will not. That is just how the cookie crumbles.

96.   **Be Prepared:** Follow the motto of the Boy Scouts and be prepared while you are writing. It is always good to have pens, pencils, paper, water, etc. nearby.

97.   **Pursue Your Interests:** Do not sacrifice your hobbies and interests at the expense of writing. Writing can become a way of life, but it should not devour your life.

98.   **Be A Knowledge Consumer:** Do not just read, but consume information. Read the newspaper, research random topics on Wikipedia, watch CNN.

99.   **Don't Be Lazy:** There is relaxing, and then there is just being plain lazy. Just walking a mile or so can do wonders, and extracurriculars can give you valuable insight into how the world works.

100.   **Be A Reporter:** A reporter always asks: Who? What? When? Where? Why? And How? You should do the same with your writing.

101.   **Talent Is Cheap. Dedicated Work Is Not:** I saved the best tip for last. There are plenty of those with lots of talent, but they spend their days playing World of Warcraft or figuring out ways to do as little work as possible and get away with it. In no matter what you do, work hard and people will take notice. This applies to writing as well. If you dedicate yourself to your stories, people will take notice.

GRAND AVENUE
Abbey M.

17 (F) of Arizona, USA

The word "diner" was one that I always misread as "dinner."

So it was a tricky issue when I sat down for lunch in a din(n)er on Grand Avenue, waiting for a man that I had never met before. His name was Ivan, a terribly trite and boring name but I could do nothing about it. But his name was pretty much all the information that I had on him. I did not know his face and I did not know what he wore or what he drove or anything. I could see out the window and watch people pull in to the diner's lot, but none of them looked at me, and none of them looked like an Ivan.

Grand Avenue, incidentally, isn't all that grand. The Phoenix valley is a grid – all the major north-south streets intersect the major east-west streets at perfect, 90 degree angles with a Walgreens on almost every corner. It is rare to find any of these intersections without some kind of business on at least one corner. America: Land of the Get-Your-Capitalism-Here.

Grand Avenue, however, runs diagonally across the valley, intersecting at a 45 degree angle and messing up the entire system. A railroad track runs next to it, and during the Japanese interment era of World War II, it had been used as part of the eastern boundary for the West coast of the country. Now it traced US Route 60 and caused a headache for many an annoyed driver used to the grid system.

I sat down for lunch in a diner on Grand Avenue in a gridlocked city, waiting for a man that I had never met, my chest clenched tight with nerves. The waitress asked me if I was ready to order. I ordered a soda and told her I had another person coming. She left without a word.

I watched the flow of traffic on the misnamed Grand Avenue. The cars stopped uniformly at the light and started again in the same fashion. It was funny to me how they all started almost exactly at the same time, and yet as one accelerated faster than the other two lanes of traffic, it pulled away like a horse at the races. Some random formula from my high school physics course floated through my head and I shook it off, suppressing the memories of that class. I had failed it with flying colours. The only thing I was good at in that class was flunking tests.

Had it been legal, I would have pulled out a cigarette and subsequently lit it up at the table. It wasn't that I actually smoked – it just felt like it would have completed the apathetic college girl mood. Something about archetypes or some other thing that English teachers are always rambling about. It just felt right, but of course I didn't have cigarettes, and even if I had, I'm sure that the waiters and other patrons would bite my head off.

So I sipped the drink that the waitress brought me and stared out the window, watching the traffic on the not-so-grand Grand Avenue in a diner in a gridlocked city. I turned as the door of the diner opened. A man walked in. He had short red hair and a square chin and a confused look. Somehow, even though I had never seen him before, I knew. This was Ivan. It must have been a result of sharing half my genetics with him. There was something connecting us in an inexplicably powerful way. I paused, my heart beating a steady tattoo against the inside of my rib cage. I thought of the cigarette to regain my composure.

He looked around, glancing at a tiny paper square that he held in his hand. I saw him chew nervously on his tongue, his lips slightly parted and his tongue extending slightly past them. He had the same nervous habit I did. He also had the same nose that I did, pointy and prolific.

He saw me. He looked at his tiny paper square, which I later discovered was his only photo of me. I thought of the cigarette.

Ivan walked over, asked me my name. I told him, in what was arguably one of the most awkward moments of my life. Unnecessarily, he said his name was Ivan. I invited him to sit down.

The silence was like a bubble, cut off from the noise of the restaurant outside of our little booth.

It was a tricky issue when I sat down for lunch in a diner on not-so-grand Grand Avenue in a gridlocked city, sipping my drink with a man I had never met but was, by the wonderful gift of genetics, my father.

"So I'm sorry to hear about your mother," he said, not meeting my eyes. I shrugged.

"It was her time, I guess," I said.

"How is school? When do you graduate high school?"

"I graduated two years ago," I said, trying to hide my shaking hands underneath the table. "I'm in college now. I'm an art major."

"Oh. Well… that's nice."

The silence was even worse than making awkward conversation, but we fell into it again, neither of us meeting the others' eyes. I stared out at Grand Avenue and he stared at the intricate tile pattern on the table, tracing it with his finger like a child. Both of us looked up when the waitress returned. Ivan ordered a root beer and a meat lover's pizza with extra cheese. I had a salad with some breadsticks. The waitress wrote it all down and walked away.

I wondered about her for a while. How many life-changing moments does she see in a day? How many people like Ivan and I come in and sit down for a meal and leave changed forever?

I wondered if she felt any kind of connection to phenomena like that. If she enjoyed her job because of it. I wonder if she could use any of our experiences in her own life.

"Waitresses should write books," I muttered to myself.

"'Scuse me?" Ivan said, looking up, one finger still tracing the outline of a blue diamond.

"Oh, nothing, just an inner monologue making it to the surface."

Silence came again, and stayed for the most part until our food arrived. Our attempts at conversation were halfhearted at best, and several times I excused myself for a bit of privacy in the restroom. The kindly waitress smiled at us as she set down our food. I smiled back at her and silently wished her a good day, hoping that she would go home with a healthy pocketful of tips.

"So you… like to draw?" Ivan asked as he pulled a slice off of his pizza. I nodded.

"I've been drawing since I was three. I learned to hold a pencil and draw with it before I learned to write my name."

You would have known this if you hadn't walked out, I thought scathingly. I bit my tongue. It wasn't fair of me to say that. And it wouldn't have helped the fact that we were trying to establish a new relationship in the wake of my mother's death. Ivan had read the obituary in the paper and hunted me down immediately. He felt that I would need a parent there to hold my hand.

He was right. I did. The awkwardness took my mind off of my mother.

Ivan continued struggling to make small talk, asking me random questions. Did I have a boyfriend, what were my grades like, who were my friends. I answered them all with closed answers. It was like playing ping-pong with a turtle. He'd hit the ball at me but when I hit it back, he would retreat into his shell. Not that he wasn't trying; it was just that conversation requires two participants. Like ping-pong.

I finished my salad and let my fork swim in the excess dressing, licking it like a spoon after a moment. Mum had told me not to do things like that, but Ivan didn't seem to mind. He pulled off another slice of pizza and laid it on his plate.

"You can help yourself to some, if you like," he said, gesturing at the pizza.

"I'm a vegetarian."

"Oh."

He retreated into his shell.

He ate two more slices and had the waitress box up the remaining four. He wiped his mouth with a napkin and finished his root beer. I watched him with one eyebrow cocked.

"What?" he said.

"You eat a lot for such a small man," I said.

"I work out."

"Play any sports?"

"Not really, just lift weights and jog every now and again."

"Watching your girlish figure?"

It was a knee-jerk response of mine. I used it to tease my best friend's roommate, who was always obsessing about his weight. He had given up soda and snacks and worked out every day. Their room constantly smelled of dirty gym socks as a result. They went through soap in the shower very quickly. My obligatory joke Christmas gifts to them were always giant boxes of soap.

The roommate usually rolled his eyes at my response. Ivan, however, found it hysterically funny and started to laugh.

"I guess you could say that," he said in between chuckles.

"So what do you do for a living?"

"I'm a firefighter."

"Really?" I said, perking up. He nodded.

"Have been for ten years."

I counted backwards. He had become a firefighter when I was nine. Mum said he had been jobless when he left just after I was born, and to the day she died professed that he still was.

There was a pause.

"Um… Ivan?" I said awkwardly. He glanced up. I didn't feel comfortable calling him Dad, and I told him as such. He nodded and said it was okay with him.

"Listen… I have a favour to ask of you," I said hesitantly. "It's a little weird… but it would help me a lot, and it'd be really easy for you."

"What is it?"

The waitress handed me the check. I paid it absentmindedly as I told him what I wanted.

He looked thoughtful as I talked, and when I finished, he nodded.

I smiled in relief.

* * *

"Where do you want me to stand?"

"Just over there. Just enough so that the sun isn't in your eyes but enough so that I'm not seeing your silhouette. Move a little bit to the left. Perfect. Put your foot up on that rock. Can you put your helmet under your arm and look down, with a tired expression on your face? Mess up your hair a little, helmet hair. Great. Now look out over the city. Keep your face like that as best you can. Now hold that position."

Ivan was wearing his firefighter's uniform, and I had thrown on my painting overalls over my jeans. I kept them and a button up work shirt in the trunk of my car at all times. I nestled behind my easel and picked up my painting palette.

We were on a mountain trail overlooking the Phoenix valley in its sprawling grid. I could see Grand Avenue cutting a swath through the otherwise regular checkerboard pattern. The downtown skyline rose up far in the distance.

"I can see my house from here," Ivan joked.

"I said keep a straight face! That means no lame jokes," I said. I had to admit – he made a great model. He held still as I painted him looking tired in a rumpled firefighter's uniform, which was a blessing for me. I usually had models that went bad or, if they were human, twitched a lot and messed up my shading. But Ivan held still.

"So what's this assignment about?" he asked.

"I have to paint a portrait of a life-changing moment," I said. "When you said you were a firefighter, I thought of the fact that you must save lives all the time. I'd consider that a life-changing moment."

"I'm flattered," he said.

"I've always liked firefighters," I rambled, still overwhelmed by the awkwardness of the whole ordeal. Never had I imagined I would be painting a portrait of a man I just met, let alone my father. "With the police, when they come, you might be in trouble or they might be there to help you. But firefighters… when a firefighter comes, they're there to help you, no matter what. You know what you're getting with a firefighter. It's a comforting thought, knowing there's an entire group of people that are there for that one purpose."

I started to put the details onto his body. Each stroke of the brush was careful and calculated. You can't take back brush strokes like you can pencil lines. It's an entirely different class of care.

Ivan didn't complain once as I lost myself in my work. He must have been roasting; it was winter and it was cooler than normal, but Phoenix is still a warm place. A Phoenix winter is roughly the equivalent of every other place in America's summer, and the weight of the firefighter's uniform probably wasn't helpful either. I supposed he didn't complain because he was used to charging into burning buildings – although on some days, that's an improvement from the hot weather outdoors.

It took quite some time, but I finally finished my portrait of Ivan. I looked up, holding the brush between my teeth and comparing my painting to the real thing. His hair was slightly longer than it should have been but it was a trivial mistake at best. I gestured to him – the universal "come hither" gesture. He obeyed, standing at my left and turning to look at the painting.

"My word," he gasped. "It's beautiful."

I smiled.

"Do you get your projects back after you turn them in?" he asked. "I'd like to hang this in my house or in the fire station, if you'd let me."

"Well, first I have to finish it, but I don't want to keep you any longer than I have to," I said. "And yes, I get them back after I get a grade, and yes, you can have it after that."

He smiled. We looked at each others' smiling faces.

I hesitated. I had thought about it, but I hadn't quite made up my mind. But my mouth had made it up for me, and the words escaped before I knew what was happening.

"Thanks, Dad," I said.

There were no words as tears sprang to his eyes and he picked me up in a big bear hug, paint splatters and all.

* * *

Two weeks later, I sat down for lunch at the same din(n)er on Grand Avenue and waited for Ivan.

This time, laying on its side on the bench next to me, was a covered painting. I patted it and smiled as I waited for Ivan to come in.

I shook my head. He wasn't Ivan to me anymore. He was Dad. I had to get used to calling him that.

He more or less skipped into the diner and sat down across from me, his face flushed and his smile wide. I smiled back and our conversation sprang up as we ordered, waited for, and consumed our food. Talking to him was no longer like playing ping-pong with a turtle. Now, it was more like playing it with the ping-pong champion of the world. I had been delighted to discover that he had the same snarky sense of humour that I did. It made talking to him all the more easier.

He paid for our meal this time, saying he had nineteen years of dinners to make up for. I told him that it wasn't necessary. He brushed my comment aside like a speck of dust.

"So, is that the finished portrait?" he said, eyeing the canvas behemoth beside me. I nodded.

"Yep. Painted, graded, and ready to go. Would you like to see it?"

"I've only been waiting two weeks to see it, why don't you hang onto it for another two?"

"Don't tempt me, mister."

We both laughed, and I stood up, taking the painting with me. I stood at the side of the table and held it up, my feet supporting the bottom and my hands steadying the upper corners.

"Ready?" I said. He nodded enthusiastically.

I pulled the canvas cover off of the painting.

He blinked, his face unreadable. I chewed my tongue.

"What happened to the portrait of me on the mountain?" he asked. "Did you... did you mess that one up or something?"

"Not exactly," I said, sitting down next to him and holding the painting up with one hand. "I had a change of heart. The assignment was to paint a life-changing moment. My original plan was to paint you walking away from a burning house with a family in the background. You had saved them from the fire, but hadn't managed to save their house. It was a nice idea and I might keep it for future references. I still have the original portrait; maybe it'll resurface at Christmas or something. But for now, this is what I turned in."

We looked at the painting. A waitress was walking away from a table with two people sitting at it – a young girl and a man approaching middle age. She was smiling, a notepad in her hand. The two people, small and miniscule in the background, looked like they were talking. But they were a relatively insignificant detail. The waitress took up most of the space, the level of detail on her making her look as if she was ready to walk straight off the canvas. She wore black slacks and a grey t-shirt with black rings on the sleeves. She had a name tag pinned to her shirt – it had the diner's logo and a blurred, eroded name. Her hair was done up in a neat bun behind her head, a few stray black strands pointing whichever direction that they pleased. Her skin was smooth and fair. Her almond-shaped brown eyes showed the very first signs of crow's feet at the corners. She was lovely in a quaint sense.

"It's beautiful," Dad said softly. I smiled.

"What did you get on it?"

"One hundred percent."

He smiled.

"I expected nothing less from my little girl."

We embraced while having lunch in a diner on Grand Avenue.

The waitress smiled at us.

TO MY UNSPOKEN NAME
Angela H.

17 (F) of New York, USA

Unthinkable thoughts can't
come into existence without being thought.
How do you learn
knowledge unknown?
I experimented with creations
neither as scientist, nor inventor,
but as lover.
Explorations with sincerity and belief
led me to hear and finally to listen.
Your name I dare not sing
was in every melody.
If words are unspeakable,
I will not speak to you.
But nothing goes unexpressed.
So I pen my forbidden feelings
write of impossible touch,
of sights I must be blind to.
I've never savored being obvious,
but with emotions so strong they are

declared to be a weakness,
in an area where my success would be
the gravest failure, I find it is
beyond me to be subtle and
silent, as is so openly, obviously,
outspokenly expected of me:

I will shout those
unspeakable words.
I'll wish on non-existent stars,
dream of the most
unobtainable things
I've never had.

"What value will there be in life
if we are not together?"

"'Tis better to have loved and lost
than never to have loved at all."

Can I, even now, at this immeasurable time,
find it impossible to speak plainly,
except with borrowed words?
I cannot.

CHRISTMAS MAGIC
Alexa O.

17 (F) of Ontario, Canada

Karen looked out the airplane window as they landed. Three hours in the air had led them to *this*. The sky was dark gray, the grass was covered by a pitiful amount of snow, especially for mid-December, and the airport was just a concrete box.

"We are now arriving at Calgary International Airport; please make sure you take all your belongings with you. Thank you for flying with us."

Her mom glanced at the carry-on bag at Karen's feet. "Do you have everything?"

"I didn't take anything out," Karen grumbled. *Why bother?* she added silently. Most of her stuff had been packed and shipped out before they had left. Moving to Calgary from Toronto, during Christmas break— after her first semester in high school. What had her parents been *thinking*? So what if Dad got a new job. Didn't anybody care about her life?

Karen slung her bag over her shoulder, catching a stray piece of paper as it fell out of a side pocket. Before stuffing it back in her bag she looked at it. It was a picture of her older brother Damien in his uniform. He was in Afghanistan now, somewhere. He never did tell them where he was, no matter how much she or her family pestered him. He said it was for safety reasons, but Karen knew he was just trying to prevent them from worrying. It wasn't working.

"Karen, let's go!" her dad's voice snapped her back to reality.

She carefully put the picture back in its place. "Coming."

* * *

Everything was unpacked just in time for Christmas Eve. Karen looked out the window in her room. She wouldn't admit it, but she liked her new room better then her old one. It was bigger, and had a window seat. The only thing missing were the shelves for all her stuffed toys. She wouldn't put that up though. Stuffed toys where for little kids, not fourteen year olds.

Snow fell gently outside. As she watched it, Karen remembered the times she and Damien had tried to stay up all night, just to catch Santa. Even though he knew the truth, he always pretended for her sake. He had done it so well, she hadn't stopped believing until this year— the year he had left.

She shook her head and crawled into bed. Believing in Santa was just a kid's dream. Something that didn't matter when you got older. It wasn't worth it. Not without somebody to share it with.

Karen turned over in the freezing sheets. A tear rolled down her cheek, but she brushed it away. *It's just the cold,* she told herself. *It's just the cold.*

* * *

For the first time in her life Karen got up at seven a.m. on Christmas day. She had always woken up Damien at three just to see if Santa had come. She bit her lip at the memory and tromped downstairs. The tree had a mountain of presents under it, most of them marked "from Santa." Karen sneered at her parents' effort. A new home, without Damien, and she was supposed to be cheered up by *Santa?* She crossed her arms as her parents came downstairs. This Christmas wouldn't matter. It just wouldn't.

Karen kept that resolve while opening presents. Manners had been drilled into her, so each gift got a murmured thank you, but that was it. She didn't stop longer then necessary until the final gift. A battered envelope, with Damien's scrawled handwriting. Most people had a hard time reading it, but Karen had never had any trouble. She could easily read the label:

To- Ren

From- Damim

Karen bit her lip. When she had been little she hadn't been able to say his name properly. He'd shortened her name to get back at her, and both had just stuck. He was the only one that called her that, mostly when he wanted to irk her, but it was nice to see it again. She was surprised he even remembered.

She put the envelope in her housecoat pocket. "Can I go to my room now?"

Her mom sighed. "Yes. Go on."

Karen ignored her parent's whispers about her as she went up the stairs. She closed the door to her room and plonked herself down on the window seat. She opened the envelope as quietly as possible and pulled the letter out. She wasn't surprised at the lack of a gift; Damien had always been horrible at picking out presents.

She read over the letter, fighting the urge to hop on a plane and go see what was going on for herself. Damien had always been good at telling them just enough that they wondered what was going on, but never enough information that they knew he was alright. It wasn't until she reached the end of the letter that she stopped fidgeting.

Well, that's everything. I hope you managed to catch Santa this year. Sorry I couldn't be there to help you with that. I always stay up later than you! I sure hope it snows sometime around Christmas in Calgary. It's just not Christmas without snow. Yes, that means it's not really Christmas here. I heard it snows only once every seven years here? You'd be the person to ask. So, does it snow every seven years here?

Just giving you a little Christmas gift. I know how much you love looking up that stuff. Hope you'll enjoy your new school. You know what they say, 'when one door closes, another opens!' And hey, maybe a little Christmas magic will rub off on your first day. All you need to do is believe.

Love,

Damien

P.S. - Keep dreaming, and keep believing! God knows, doing that has saved my sanity. But, that shouldn't be a problem for you.

Karen rubbed her eyes, feeling her finger slide over dampness. But it is a problem. *How can you dream, when your belief is gone?*

Slowly she got up and put the letter on her nightstand. She went to her closet and dug under her out-of-season clothes to pull out the last unopened box. Karen picked up a pair of scissors from her desk and cut the packing tape.

Inside the box were her favourite stuffed toys— the ones that had been on her shelf. She took them out and lined them up on her desk. The last toy in the box she placed front and center. Damien had given her that stuffed bear to protect her at night. Karen smiled at the thought she had believed that once upon a time. She was about to put the toy nearer the end of her desk when she stopped. She ran her fingers over the worn fur, remembering all the times she had hugged it and felt better. Karen hugged it again now. For a moment, just a moment, she felt Damien's arms around her. She sighed and put the bear down, wishing he could be here to give her a hug for real.

The smell of pancakes wafted in from under her door. It looked like her mom was making her traditional Christmas pancakes. Karen remembered in Toronto, she and Damien would help her make them. This Christmas wasn't supposed to matter though. But, they had always had so much fun...

Slowly Karen went into the hall and back downstairs.

"Need any help?"

* * *

Another week went by, and Christmas break was over. Karen resented having her mom drive her to school; in Toronto she could have just taken the bus.

She made her way through the school to homeroom. There was an empty seat in the middle row, by the window. As Karen put her stuff down the teacher came in and asked her to introduce herself. Karen felt her cheeks turn red as she stood at the front of the class and said her name like a preschooler.

When she was finished, the teacher stood up. "Karen, since you're the newest student, perhaps you'd like to share your favourite Christmas memory."

Karen bit her lip. It seemed her homeroom teacher was also the creative writing teacher. "Well, my brother and I used to stay up and try to catch Santa. We never did though."

A kid in class snorted. "You don't really believe in Santa, do you?"

Karen was about to snap back that she didn't, when Damien's letter popped into her mind. Hadn't he told her to believe?

"Yes, I do believe."

She ducked her head at the onslaught of laughter from the classroom. Exactly the same thing would have happened in Toronto, had she ever said she still believed in Santa at thirteen. But it felt good to say it, even if she would be the laughing stock of the school for the next four years.

A girl at the back stood up. "Can I add something, Ms. Morin?"

The teacher nodded. "You may Becky."

"Well, um," Becky looked at Karen, then straitened her shoulders. "I believe in Santa too."

Silence fell over the class. Karen smiled and went back to her seat. She glanced over her shoulder to Becky and waved slightly. Maybe, Damien was right. When one door closes, another opens, and Karen liked the door that had opened.

Karen turned to the front of the class, half-listening to the teacher talk about what would happen this year. She kept thinking about Damien, and how he would have been proud. She'd have to drop him a line and tell him about her first day of school.

As everybody left the classroom, Karen heard somebody behind her whisper,

"You don't *really* believe in Santa, do you? That stuff's for little kids!"

She turned to face him, a smile spreading across her face. "Yes, I really do."

MOTHER
Conrad R.

19 (M) of Oklahoma, USA

"So, what are we going to do?" Ted asked Brant.

"Does it really matter?" She shrugged her shoulders.

"Well, yeah," Ted said. "I mean, when something like that shows up in your backyard claiming to be your mother, you don't just say, 'Oh, come on in Momma. Be careful. Don't let your hooves track in mud.'"

Brant looked out the window into the yard. She was still out there. A trim, pale woman's body above, with no clothing to hide her elegant features. Below, a muscular, dark horse's body, without any sign of domestication. She was cast in a strange light by the stars and moon, the stark contrast of her two parts enhancing her beauty, complementing her very well. It was a picture right out of mythology, or a work of poetry even. She took Brant's breath away. Such things shouldn't even exist. And yet there she was in all her power and glory.

"Why not?" she asked. Ted's eyes went wide with disbelief.

"Why not? Isn't it obvious? It shouldn't even exist!"

"Don't talk about her like that," Brant said, rebuking her brother without even a second thought.

"You're nuts, off your rocker," Ted said. "I don't know how you can believe that thing. We've got actual birth certificates; we know who our mother is."

"There isn't a video though," Brant said. "We don't know for sure."

"Just because Mom's coming down a little hard on you for that stunt you pulled last week doesn't give you the right to go saying that she's not your real mother."

"All I did was spend the night at the barn," Brant said. "Lea was foaling, I had to be there for her, to comfort her. And besides, that has nothing to do with this. That's not why I'm saying that we should believe her. It's because she feels like our real mother."

"There we go again," Ted said. He shook his head. "You and your feelings. Forget logic, forget rational thought, we'll go with feminine feelings. That's sure to help us along."

"Ted, you're not helping."

"Well, neither are you. You're so caught up with her and what she is you can't see what's real and what's not anymore."

Brant turned to her brother, searching for some explanation of what he had said.

"Caught up?" she asked. "Just how am I caught up?"

"You're always talking about how you just, 'feel right,' when you're at the barn, when you're around the horses. You blog about how you feel a kindred spirit with them all the time."

"You read my blog?" Brant's eyes went wide with outrage. "That's private!"

"It's on the internet, total strangers read it, it's not that private," Ted replied. "But that's beside the point. The point is that here's a chance for you to explain those feelings, hell, to act on them. Here is your dream, and you're ready to fall head over heels into it based on that. Never mind the facts; it's appealing, so you're gonna do it."

Brant turned away and looked out the window again. The creature in the yard was looking up at the window; up at her. Her eyes spoke of longing, a mother's longing, Brant thought. No, she didn't think it, she knew it. How could Ted not see it?

"You're not even listening, are you?" he asked.

"Why does it even matter if she's our mother?" Brant asked him. "We just keep her fed and tell her our problems. She'll be all about us. Even you're not too dense to see how much she cared about us."

"But in the end, it won't be just that," Ted said. "She cares that much, she's not going to just want a little time with us. It'll be more and more time, until finally she runs off with us. We don't need that."

The creature pawed at the ground with a nervous air. Brant put a hand to the window, letting a slow breath fog up the glass. What Ted said played in her mind like an echo in a canyon. But she couldn't be sure that what he said was true. Did she really need to stay here? Did she really not need to be carried away? Something told her that wasn't the case. Something told her that she needed to be with family, to be what she really was. The creature looked up at the window again. Brant smiled down at her, a special smile, one that spoke whole books about her actions. The creature smiled back.

THE STARRY SKY
Christiana G.

21 (F) of New Jersey, USA

There was a bed
covered by a quilt
with two sides.

One side was dark blue,
spotted with dots
of silver and gold.

The other side was
a lighter blue with
hazy white shapes.

The pillow sat at
the head of the bed,
inviting one to slumber.

Its cover mimicked
the quilt, glowing
silver blue with the dark.

Light blue and white
bring about gold,
orange, and red.

Stuffed animals were
hidden throughout
the blue bed.

Behind the pillow, under
the covers: it would take
a keen eye to spot them.

Different animals, with
many shapes and feels,
to comfort those in need.

All these things make
the bed a perfect place
for relaxation and dreams.

TO LOVE
Holly H.

14 (F) of New Mexico, USA

Sometimes I feel incomplete. Often, it feels like a big chunk of my world broke off and floated away to make its own peaceful, quiet place. But now there is two unfinished pieces floating around in space, searching for the other in vain. There is no turning back now.

Exactly six months ago, my twin sister died. She is the missing piece of my world. We were closer than anyone else ever even came close to. I loved her so much. But I didn't find out just how much I really did love her until she was already gone.

My family and I are driving to Rock Hill Cemetery, where my sister rests. We go every month on the day she died—the ninth. I'm sitting in the back of the car, observing the faces of my family. In the seat to my right, my brother Samuel looks down at his lap and twirls his thumbs sadly. In the passenger's seat, my mother sets her jaw like she's trying to be strong. But the tear rolling down her cheek doesn't escape my attention. Through the rearview mirror, I can see my dad's sorrowful gray eyes fixed blindly on the road ahead. I turn to the window I'm sitting in and look at my reflection. Sad, puffy eyes stare back at me, their pupils islands lost in a sea of hopelessness. I press my hand on the frosty window. Another milky, transparent hand touches the tips of my fingers on the outside of the car.

I miss you.

The car turns and the light moves, taking my reflection with it.

Goodbye.

I wonder if she has forgotten me. She probably has too much fun in heaven to pay any attention to what's going on down on Earth. I wonder if she still helps others like she helped me, distraught souls that are confused and sad. I wonder if she's troubled too, like them, or if she's living her new life in blissful ignorance. Why did God have to take her away from me? Would He let her forget about me?

I focus outside, where the sun makes the powdery snow sparkle brighter than any precious stone. The pine trees droop under the weight of the snow, mourning. Ruddy-cheeked children play in the snow, laughing. They don't know that the saddest girl in the world was passing them at that very moment.

Tears burn my eyes. The scene outside has changed—rows of lifeless slabs of stones darting past. They seem so cruel and heartless. They are gray and cold like the weather.

The car stops. I grab the flowers perched in the middle seat and step out. My boots sink into the soft snow, swallowing my foot whole. We all trudge slowly past graves. Some have large crosses on the top; others are just curved stone. Some have beautiful, smiling angels. But their smiles are bitter and apathetic. I see her tombstone immediately. It is smaller and simpler than all the ones around her. How she deserved so much more than all the rest of these dead people.

CAMERON BAILEY

1995-2007

I set the bouquet of her favorite flowers next to her gravestone. A gust of wind blows a tattered, yellow paper at my feet. A small voice in my heart tells me that this paper is very important. I slowly bend down, my family staring at me curiously. I smooth it out a little on my knee, hold it up, and read it in my head.

To love is to not forget. You will never be forgotten by those whom loved you.

God will never let her forget me.

NOTHING RHYMES WITH PURPLE
David B.

15 (M) of Blenheim, New Zealand

Nothing rhymes with purple,
Lament, for it is true,
Cause' who would take the time, to rhyme,
With colours such as blue?

Dr Seuss could rhyme with purple,
His literary master plan,
Was rhyme purple using flurple,
And other words unknown to man.

But alas, for he's not with us now,
Purple rhyming's moved on too,
I know y'all care, but don't despair,
Rhyming will indeed, get through.

We can try to rhyme with purple,
Keep alive this rhyming craze,
Don't let it die, you have to try,
You may well be amazed!

They say nothing rhymes with purple,

But we know now that's not true,

But who'd "waste" time, on such a rhyme?

Just Dr Seuss, that's who!

FIRST KISS

Cassaundra E.

16 (F) of Washington, USA

It's a pretty restaurant. We had picked a back table in a nook, further away from the people, and where the candle was almost brighter than the chandelier. The waitress comes by with the check, asking if we want any dessert.

"No, but thank you," he smiles. She smiles back at both of us and puts the check on the table before slipping away.

He turns to face me. He's handsome, has the smile you would see on a magazine. Gorgeous guy. I bite my lip and hide my hands under the table, worried I might knock something over. I'm clumsy and average looking. Normally, the former was an annoyance and the latter didn't matter. But what if I knocked over my glass, spilt ice water over both of us, or worse, just him? Everything on the table looked like a disaster ready to happen. Why did he agree to a date?

Maybe because he's great, and he doesn't care that I'm younger and odd-looking.

He has a car as well as the legal right to drive it. I'm still learning the laws of the road. And he's almost a year older. My eyes pursue every decorative swirl on the wall paper, trying to determine if they're all the same. A year older. He's probably kissed lots of girls. I've yet to be kissed by any other than my family. What is he thinking of me? He's staring at me. Does he think I'm a cheap ticket? Or does he not care about the age and beauty difference? Would he have said yes to a date otherwise? I twist my ring around on my finger nervously and look back at him.

He leans forward carefully, like he's nervous, too. He looks like he's asking a question, like he's inviting me to lean forward with him. I do, but only a little, no more than he had. Don't make assumptions. He smiles and leans closer. He wants to kiss me, I think to myself. He wants to kiss me.

I hesitate a moment as a barrage of questions attack my mind. I take a breath and lean forward again until I can feel his breath on my chin. Would it be slobbery? Harry Potter said it was wet. Or dry-ish? Soft and electric? Gentle and intimate? I close my eyes, trying to stop questioning this moment so I can enjoy it. Our lips are almost touching, there's hardly any air between us. Was it true that you couldn't breathe during a kiss, a real kiss? What if I couldn't hold my breath as long as him and I jerk away gasping for air? That would be horrible and very unromantic. I feel his hand brush my cheek, I feel him coming closer, his nose grazing mine as he tilts his head to the side…and begins licking my face in long, slobbery laps. I jump back and shove him away.

"What are you *doing?*" I demand. He only barks and starts licking my face again.

My eyes snapped open in disgust. Groaning at the all-to-familiar goop on my face, I shoved my dog off of me. Normally, I didn't have a problem with Sandy's wake-up methods. It was just in moments like these when I hate them. Sandy fell off the bed with a thump. Not at all fazed by her fall, she just jumped back up to thoroughly bathe my face in dog slobber.

"Knock it off. See? Speaking. I'm up." And when Sandy continued to fill my ear with slime, "Go get food," I said, flinging my hand in the general direction of the door.

At the mention of food, Sandy was off, claws clapping on the hard wood floor as she raced to the kitchen. I threw my head back in my pillow, muttering a few of Tolkien's dwarven curses as I futilely tried to reclaim the already-lost dream.

PHOTONS, EXCITE!
Karina O.

21 (F) of California, USA

look at me and rejoice!
see my hair, how it sparkles in the sun
and transforms into spindles of gold for you.
and look! when you touch my cheek with
the back of your hand,
can't you feel soft rosy petals pressed
against your flesh?
remember me like this, i pray, and don't let
my driver's license fool you.
my hair is *not* brown and my skin is *not* white.
how could it be? listen!
in darkness, i was nothing,
but then God said, "let there be light!"
and i tumbled from my mother's womb and
blinked.

when you see me now, what you see is
not me but a billion photons dancing
with my molecules.

i am in God and God is in me –
even my sweater with the holey sleeve
throbs with the pulse of raging electrons,
all in the tune of God's song.

(and when i kiss you, God laughs and
a thousand and one stars twinkle.)

ASSISTANCE IN ENDINGS
Matthew D.

17 (M) of Westport, New Zealand

"When did you first notice his symptoms?" the man asked, fidgeting with the collar of his white coat. His eyes stayed fixed on Emma and I, ignoring the murmuring presence of our child behind us.

I opened my mouth to answer, but Emma cut in before me. "When he was very young. We noticed that he wasn't progressing as fast as the other children he played with. But we thought we'd wait before we did anything drastic about it." Her high heeled foot tapped against the wooden floor while her hand beat a rhythm on her thigh. "When he was nearly two and he still wasn't saying more than a few words, we knew something was wrong." Her voice stayed clipped and detached, speaking at a steady rate.

"And he's three years old now?" the man said, looking down at a clipboard. *Dr. Roberts*, his nametag read. He was one of those people with an intense gaze that bored into you. I don't know how anyone with a face like that could be a paediatrician.

Danny sat on the floor and watched us speak. Watched *them* speak, more like. It's not like I contributed anything to that conversation.

"Yes. We should have brought him in sooner. I always said so, but Dave said to give it some time." She turned to look at me, but I kept my gaze fixed on the ground. "He said if we waited long enough he might come right."

The doctor smiled at us. "It's okay, Mr. Gordon. Yours was a perfectly normal reaction. Half the patients I see have delayed their visit for months, sometimes years. It's even harder with a child.

"The test results are back, and I'm sorry to say, they aren't very good. Danny has Down syndrome. It's one of the more severe cases that I've seen, which means that it's going to be tough. I won't go into detail, but I've got some information here for you. It's a lot to digest, so read in your own time." He took a stack of papers and handed them to Emma. "With some guidance, he could have a fairly normal life. He'll never be completely independent, but he could at least start school and grasp some basic concepts. We'll need further tests to see the full extent of his disability, but we'll do them another day. He's been through enough."

Emma had her arms crossed in her lap. "Okay."

I looked up at him. "Is there – is there any chance that you've misdiagnosed him?"

"I'm afraid not. I'm sorry, but your son has Down syndrome. It isn't really as bad as it seems. Some sufferers, even those with severe cases, live fairly normal lives."

The doctor stood. Emma followed suit. I stared down at Danny before picking him up. Dr. Roberts opened a drawer and retrieved a bright purple lollipop and removed its wrapper. He held it out to Danny. "Here you go. Would you like a lollipop?"

"We don't like him to have too much sugar," Emma said.

"One won't make a difference," I said, taking the lollipop and handing it to Danny. "There you go, buddy. What do you say?"

"Thank you," Danny said, swaying from side to side and sucking on the lollipop. That was a habit of his. He never stopped moving. Even when you put him in bed, his toes would wriggle.

"Big boy's voice, Danny."

"He's never going to be a big boy, Emma," I said, sighing. A deluge of lost opportunities and dreams of the future flashed before my eyes, washed away by a flood of despair. Gone were the fantasies of my son being a lawyer, a doctor, an astronaut. He would be lucky to stack shelves in a supermarket. Emma glared, but I didn't look away. "We'd better go."

Emma shook the doctor's hand. "Thank you, Doctor." *Thank you? Thanks for crushing our last hopes, Doctor.* I blinked back tears, managing to keep the floodgates closed. I carried Danny to the car and strapped him into the car seat, planting a kiss on his forehead before closing his door.

"You can drive," I said to Emma. "I'm not up to it." My joints creaked as we got in and drove away, stiff from an eternity in the office. Every few minutes, I turned to look at Danny. My chest hurt every time I saw him smiling back at me. Eventually I stopped, resting my head against the seat.

"Don't do that again," Emma said.

"What?" I said, lifting my head from the seat and staring at her. Her lips were pursed, her eyes narrowed. There were wrinkles congregating around her eyes. *You used to be so beautiful,* I thought. Age hadn't killed her beauty, though. It was my perception. Everything fades, and you're left to wonder what happened.

"Undermine me like that. You know that I don't want him having sugar. He keeps us awake all night."

"I wasn't undermining you. I was letting him have a treat. I think he deserved it."

"Okay. I don't want an argument. But we need to have a united front."

She kept her eyes fixed on the road as I glanced at her. Her back was perfectly straight, even the smallest expression caged. Even when we hold our grief inside, it manifests itself physically somehow.

We arrived home soon after. Our house was a vivid yellow two story. Usually its brightness made me feel sick, but on that day its colours seemed bland.

The sun was starting to set now, purple swirls catching my eye as I took Danny from the seat. I pointed them out. "Look, Danny. Isn't that a pretty sunset?" His hands reached out to stroke the dazzling oranges and purples.

"Yes, Daddy."

"I'll take you upstairs and we'll read a book. Then it's bedtime, okay?"

"Okay."

"Good boy," I said as we stepped inside.

"I'm going to bed," Emma said. "My head hurts. Night, Danny."

"Night, Mummy." She kissed him and headed upstairs.

"Story time!"

"Story time!" he cried.

He ran up the dark mahogany stairs in front of me. I made sure to keep a few steps below in case he fell. As we ascended, light grew sparse. Shadows lengthened, their fingers grasping for Danny.

"Daddy, open the gate!" I opened the latch and swung the gate wide so that he could step through. We'd baby-proofed the house months before Danny was born, and had never gotten rid of it.

"Right, go find a book you want to read."

He raced to the bedroom. When I got there, he was already in the bed, holding the book out to me.

I sat down on the bed beside him and began to read. After I finished, I put the book down and looked at Danny. His eyes were already half closed. "Did you enjoy that, Danny?"

"Yes!"

"We'll have another story tomorrow night. Bedtime now."

"Drink first?"

"Okay. Come on, we'll grab a glass of water."

He jumped out of bed. I watched as he danced towards the door and smiled. A thought struck me as I placed the book back on its shelf. *Will I have to read him a bedtime story every night, until I can't even look after myself?*

I felt the tears beginning to well once again. Danny's body would grow while his mind stayed the same. He would be a child trapped in an adult's body for the rest of his life. *How can I force someone to live like that? What kind of life could it be? Why should he have to face the stigma, the pain, the alienation? Who'll look after him once we die?*

I shook my head. "Stop it."

"What, Daddy?"

"Nothing."

"Okay."

"I love you, Danny." My throat felt raw.

"Love you too."

I walked to the staircase. Danny was waiting at the gate. My knees began to shake. *How can you force him to live this fake life? How can you live with yourself?*

I gritted my teeth. "Come on!" he said, tapping his foot. "Open the gate!"

I reached over to open the latch. He hesitated on the top step. *Do it,* said a voice in my head. I was a silent spectator, watching as my own hand reached out and tipped Danny over the edge.

For a few seconds, his arms wind-milled. It was as if time stood still. I had made a decision that I could never take back. He didn't make a noise as he overbalanced, rolling over a million times; each step inviting a new crunch, a snap of bones. He twisted in ways that I could never have imagined, a grotesque contortionist. Then it was over. His body lay motionless.

The body, I thought. I looked at him, skin already beginning to pale.

Emma's shriek echoed from the bedroom. I found myself answering with a scream of my own. A single thought enveloped my mind.

Danny, forgive me.

I Write In The Dark
Sam R.

22 (F) of Northants, England

I write in the dark because
My hands have nocturnal eyes.
They think and feel for themselves
And see in the dark when I cannot.

I can barely make out the lines
And the words I have written are
Probably slanted and meshed together.
I wonder if it will all be legible tomorrow.
I'm sure it will still be in my head tomorrow.

I write in the dark because
My mind is an attic of old thoughts,
Wishful thinking, memories and worries,
Stacked up in boxes thick with dust
And too heavy to clear away.

The black of the attic is full and deep,
But empty and void of complications.

There is nothing to see, so my hands
Plunge into the boxes, finding new things.

I write in the dark because
I do not need my eyes to see.
The spill of thoughts on the paper reveals
Sometimes in the attic, my hands
Discover things I didn't know were there.

THE MAGIC FLUTE
Jennifer R.

18 (F) of Missouri, USA

Tuesday, May 10

It's not just black notes.

It's a whole different language.

Billy's sister said that so many times, he had the lines memorized with her voice too: her screechy, high-pitched voice. Once she would come home from school, he would run out for a burger. He had no need for an entire lesson on breath support or expression. At this rate, he could pick up a bassoon and join the orchestra.

Like that would ever happen.

He sat in the bleachers of the high school gym, racing neck-and-neck with Princess Peach and attempting to shove her pretty pink kart off the side. Despite Wario's size, his kart could not roll over Peach's vehicle. Both his arms tensed, and his teeth ground together until they were out of alignment and a retainer would be working heavy-duty that night. Eventually, in his excitement, he kicked the woman in front of him who, as casually as she could, looked over her shoulder. He jerked his head in a "What's up?" fashion, and his mom jabbed him in the side.

"Sit still," she hissed. "Your sister's about to play. You should listen."

Billy snorted and returned to his game. Peach bumped his kart off the side, knocking him from second to last place. "Oh, no you don't, Princess," he whispered. He started his kart, nabbed the power-up on the road, and burst down the road.

"While the symphonic band warms up in the band room," said the girl on the gym floor, "we're going to have a couple soloists perform for us. All four people playing tonight received *top scores* at the solo and ensemble competition last weekend. Let's give them a hand!" The audience applauded lightly; Billy could feel his mom getting antsy. "First up is Katie Fischer!"

The audience applauded as Billy's sister walked onto the floor. Billy watched her set up. Katie handed the piano accompanist the music, and then set her own on the stand. Raising it to her height and blowing into her flute to warm it up, she took her time in preparation for a fantastic performance…again. Uninterested, Billy returned to his Nintendo DS.

The piano started, a trickle of notes flowing into one ear, through his head, and out the other. He heard this song way too many times to even give an *ounce* of care.

When Katie hit the top note she countless times messed up in some way, Billy looked up. Even while she played, Billy could see the pride etched in her face. That note still hung in the air, ringing eternally into the night. It would never be forgotten; he could already hear the compliments she would get afterward.

With that sickening thought, Billy returned to his game. He growled quietly when he found him sitting in the lake this time, off the road and in last place. Clicking a few buttons and options, the race was reset. *1…2…3…Go!*

And he went.

Katie hit another note she had struggled with before. He ground his teeth and prevented himself from looking up. He would *not* let Peach beat him. A red, spiky shell was flung at him from behind, but Billy dodged it. He left a pile of nails as he drove away, and Mario was sent flying to the sideline. Peach knocked him to the side though, and Billy was reset again —last place and right behind Mario.

"Billy, you're going to hurt someone again," his mom muttered to him.

"Nah, I'm fine," Billy managed to say. He leaned to the right as his character turned to the right, bumping into his mom. She jabbed him fiercely in the thigh, and he winced. "Ah! Sorry, okay?" He did not look at her but at the screen, passing up Bowser.

Katie ended on her last note. Billy looked up and watched her sweat as she held the note out long and quietly. He remembered her complaining how hard it was to decrescendo a high note. It could not be that hard, but here she was, shaking to the very last second that she let go. The audience did not listen to it echo off the walls and vanish. They clapped loudly and proudly. Billy's mom stood up, frantically applauding and waving at her daughter as she left the gym.

Billy hadn't noticed.

He stared blankly at the screen, not pressing any buttons. Without a player, Wario drove straight ahead into the lake. The game reset him on the road, but Wario didn't go. He stayed put—as did Billy.

Billy felt his head spin, but he couldn't feel his fingers. His sister continued to hold the note as the room whirled around him—or did he whirl around in it?—and his body fell limp on the bleachers.

His mom heard him fall. Her proud face changed abruptly to a frightened look. Leaning over him and shaking him, she shouted his name. "Billy? Billy! Wake up! What's wrong, Billy?"

Billy heard her shout, but all he could do was knock on the Nintendo screen.

Dear Dori,

Tonight didn't go as well as I'd hoped it would. My solo went much better than I thought, so that was awesome! Right after I finished, I was thinking how funny it would be to rub my accomplishment in Billy's face. He said yesterday that chances are I wouldn't play well tonight. Well, he thought wrong!

But then, when I came back in the gym with the band, a bunch of police and doctors were running around. Supposedly my brother...died? I can't believe it. My mom was a wreck, and she still is. My dad turned off the tape as soon as he noticed Billy's body, so we couldn't watch what happened. Laura's mom had the film running still though, but only because she's slow to noticing things. I should ask for a copy.

I guess I won't be rubbing anything in Billy's face. I have a lesson next week too. I wonder what Julie will say when I tell her. Maybe I can avoid it...but that wouldn't be right. Gah, I'm so confused, Dori! My brother died, and no one knows why. <u>Why</u>? I'm going to get so much crap tomorrow at school. Thanks, Billy. I know you hated my music, but was dying really worth it?

I'll tell you about tomorrow, Dori. It'll be full of interesting things anyway.

— Katie

Wednesday, May 11

"Dude, is Trace around?"

"No, he's in his office still."

"Sweet." Andrew whipped out his phone and pulled out its keyboard. His friend peered over his shoulder, but Andrew shrugged him away. "Space, dude. I need space."

"Right, sorry," Todd said and shrunk back.

They were sitting in their favorite corner of the band room—near the jazz equipment. First hour was only being wasted because Mr. Trace decided to give them a day off after the concert. No one complained.

Andrew's eyes darted up to Katie, who was concentrating on the music in front of her, and wondered if he should really do it. It wouldn't hurt to try. He's been thinking about it for a long time, and with her brother dead, she'll be in a needy state, looking for comfort and all that.; so who's going to be there for her? Andrew. That's who. But he didn't want her to hate him for eternity if the offer failed....Psh, what was he thinking? He clicked his phonebook.

"Dude, who're you texting?" Jack asked from across the circle. He sat with his chair backwards, his arms lying on the top of the back. Jack followed Andrew's gaze to Katie on the opposite side of the room. Her brow scrunched together and determination etched in her face; she was one of about five students who were actually practicing their instrument. Katie's sounded more impressive as usual. Jack looked back at Andrew, shaking his head. "You really can't be serious, Drew."

"I'm dead serious," he muttered mindlessly. His thumbs stopped pressing buttons, and he slid the keyboard back into place. He looked at Jack's disbelieving gaze. "She's really cool, dude."

"She's worthless. All she does is play her flute. She's not exciting at all. I remember when I asked to use her tuner, and she cussed me out and said that only the flutes could use it." The guys chuckled and made rude comments. "She's got problems."

"Dude, she's freaking awesome," Andrew said. "She may be moody at times, but all girls are. Me and Katie always talk about video games 'cause she likes to play too. She may not play as much as Billy, but she can play; and she likes to play." Andrew looked up at Katie and saw her toss a black phone back into her purse. His phone vibrated at that moment, and he opened it.

Not on your life, lover boy.

"That's probably just an act," Jack replied with a shrug. Andrew texted back as he spoke. "She's pretty good at acting, even if she says she's not. The drama club would be all over her if they knew her. Just drop it." He cocked his brow as Andrew read his phone again, and he snorted. "Wha'd she say? Oh, dude! Do you guys notice her mustache? Oh, my God." The guys laughed and started mocking Katie.

His phone vibrated again as Katie's flute began playing. She must have been done texting him because she started on a complicated run of sixteenth notes, plucking through the difficult parts of it and tuning notes that sounded off, but Andrew tried to ignore her. He read her message: *Shut-up or I'll have my flute shove your face into your phone.*

"Dude, you okay?" Jack asked.

Andrew closed his eyes and took a deep breath, setting his phone on his lap.

Jack snorted. "You wouldn't like her. Go ask Linda or Sara. At least they're *hot.*"

A high note rang through the air and the flute sang its best; people looked at her, some rolling their eyes and others impressed. It contained all good qualities: tone, vibrato, intonation—Andrew found himself looking up at Katie's face. She made it look difficult, but the flute couldn't have been that hard to play. Not like trumpet, for Pete's sake.

"Dude, Drew, chillax," Jack said, jerking his chin up. Todd nudged him in the shoulder, trying to regain his attention. "Just try again later. Her brother freaking died. Drew. *Drew.*"

"Oh, God," said another guy, jumping from his chair. The rest of the guys did just as well, causing alarm through the entire band room. Everyone turned toward them, but not everyone could see Andrew's lifeless body. A crowd gathered around them with gasps and screams, and Mr. Trace forced his way through the crowd.

"Someone get Mrs. Thompson," he said urgently. He tried to remain calm for the class' sake, but his eyes proved that false. "Tell her we have a medical emergency and need the nurse immediately." A girl and her friend ran for the choir room. He knelt beside Andrew and shook him lightly, calling out his name. The body didn't budge though.

Todd noticed Andrew's phone lying next to him, the screen alight as if someone pressed a button and woke it up. He reached for it, and then jumped back, horrified at whom he saw smacking the phone screen from inside.

Dear Dori,

The school's haunted, I swear. In first hour, I was just practicing my flute as I usually did during test days. (By the way, I aced that scales test no problem!) I couldn't stop thinking about Billy though. (The funeral's in a couple days.) I just felt worse. Laura said I shouldn't have played my flute. Why didn't I listen to her? She's <u>*always*</u> *right.*

I was eventually distracted by a text from Andrew. Why did I give him my number anyway? I mean, yeah, it was for a Spanish project, but I could've contacted him through someone else. Whatever. Anyway, he texted me and asked me out. I remember the text exactly: "i no u feel crapy, but wanna go out w/ me?" Aha, no. First off, I don't date people who can't even <u>*type*</u> *English with their* <u>*thumbs*</u>*; and secondly, you irritate the crap out of me. He wouldn't stop texting me after that. I got so frustrated with him; I wanted to shoot myself.*

But just like with Billy, he was just suddenly… <u>*dead*</u>*. It was the weirdest thing though. Todd showed me his phone, and Andrew was…* <u>*in*</u> *it? I freaked out. I don't know how to explain it though. He was banging on the screen, screaming for someone to help him. I mean, what could we do? If that's really Andrew, how can we get him out? As far as I know, he's stuck there forever.*

But I went a step further and checked Billy's DS. Mom said he was playing it during the concert (as he usually did). It was a stupid hypothesis, but it didn't hurt checking. And I do like Mario Kart. Not gonna lie.

It just so happened though that Billy was in the game. He begged me to get him out just like Andrew did, but all I could do was shrug. (Supposedly, they can't hear me speak. I can't hear them though, so it kind of makes sense.) So yeah, the school's haunted. A lot of people've said they're not coming to school tomorrow. Mom is still making me go, but I don't care. I'm going anyway. I'll tell you about it.

— Katie

Thursday, May 12

"My brother's dead, Lauren. My *brother*. And now Andrew."

Lauren put her arms around Katie. They've been friends since sixth grade—they met in band class, of course—and even though Katie's become a tad more annoying, Lauren wouldn't leave her alone during times like these.

"My brother's gone." Tears sprinkled her eyelashes now. Lauren rocked her gently and peered out the window of the practice room. The flute section looked so empty without Katie and her. Lauren started to regret all those terrible thoughts she had of Katie and wanted to make up for them by giving her friend an amusing and fun band class as the flutes usually had.

"Lauren, what if other people die?" Katie left Lauren's embrace and looked at her with a helpless look, a tear trickling down her cheek. "My mom is a devoted servant of God, but there is no God; otherwise, this wouldn't be happening to me."

"That's not true," Lauren put in straight away. She wanted to say more, but her arguments wouldn't really make Katie feel better. "God loves you, and I do too. You know what? We should just skip school today and sit in this practice room doing nothing. *Nothing.* We would, like…party or something. What d'you say?" Lauren smiled and laughed at her own idea, and Katie hiccupped with a watery smile.

"I have a Spanish project to do," Katie said with a sigh. "A Spanish project to do without Andrew."

"Well, then you go through the day and not worry about a thing," Lauren said. "Your brother wouldn't want you to give up just because—"

"Yeah, he would," Katie said and more tears filled her eyes. "He never cared."

"He did, but he could only show it by not caring. It's confusing, I know." Lauren hugged her again. "Don't lose hope, alright? You go make me proud and make it through school."

Katie smiled again and nodded. "I will."

"Anytime." There was silence as Katie recovered from her breakdown. When she looked to be alright, Lauren suggested, "Let's head back in, ja?"

Katie nodded, and they both left the practice room. The band fell silent as the two flutes walked in and resumed their seats. Mr. Trace kept critiquing what the band just played before finally saying, "Alright, put that up and pull out Sousa."

Lauren dug in her folder and pulled out her pile of music, flipping through each song until she found Sousa's march. Katie didn't bother pulling out her music, which Lauren didn't argue with. They would her music.

Lauren thought class went fairly well considering the recent events until Trace focused on the flute section. They played their parts for him, and Trace nailed the first flute's horrible intonation. Katie pulled out her tuner and adjusted to what it said. Lauren tuned next, but no adjustment was needed. Katie's eyes flamed, but she said nothing.

"Let's hear it again."

They played their note, and it sounded better, though not perfect. The second flutes joined in and finally the piccolo until Trace found it acceptable and moved on. Her piccolo friend Mariah poked Lauren's knee and they leaned in towards each other.

"Katie did *not* look happy with you," Mariah whispered.

"I noticed, but it's not exactly my fault," Lauren said.

"I know it isn't, but it's just…you know…"

"Yeah, I know."

"What are you guys talking about?" Katie asked.

Lauren shrugged and said, "Nothing, really."

"That's what you say every time I ask. What are you talking about? Or is it about me?" Lauren looked at her like she was crazy. The rest of the band either snickered or cursed Katie. "You two are always whispering to each other, but you never let me in on the conversation."

"Maybe they're discussing over fingerings or trills. Flutes have that stuff in this music," Mr. Trace said, trying to save Lauren and Mariah. "Plus, they're sitting next to each other. The only people one can talk to are the people they're sitting next to. They're doing nothing wrong."

"It's irritating though," Katie muttered, folding her arms across her chest.

"Katie, calm down," Lauren said as gently as she could beneath her frustration. "Just before, you were feeling alright."

"So, I'm overreacting?" Katie summed up for Lauren, taking offense.

"Just a tad."

"It's a yes or no question."

"Why do you care right now? Remember Billy? And Andrew?"

"Am I overreacting?" Katie repeated. "I know what your answer is, but a true friend would be honest, especially right now. *We've* been friends for ages. Am I overreacting?"

Lauren straightened and dared to cross the line. "Yes, you're overreacting. Now please be quiet so we can continue with class. Thank you."

Katie fell silent but turned sharply in her chair to face her music. Mr. Trace hesitated before saying the band should play from the top. Lauren could feel the band cheering for her and laughing; Mariah nudged her and shot her eyebrows up; she was just as irritated as her friend.

Lauren could hear Katie trying to outplay her, so Lauren held back. She wasn't as good as Katie anyway: Katie was first chair, and Lauren was section leader. Of course, since freshman year, the band knew nothing good would come out of the two. Now that they had their first real fight, who knew what would happen?

"Lauren!"

"Oh, my God."

Mr. Trace bounded to the phone and called the nurse. Mariah and the flutes surrounded their friend in hopes that she would, by chance, be alive. Some students crowded around them while others stayed in their seats and started talking.

Katie didn't move from her seat but stared at the mass of people in front of her. She was stiff, refusing to move, but tears streamed down her face. Katie's eyes drifted to the stand and the Sousa music, watching Lauren run and climb along the staff and notes in desperate search of a way out.

Dear Dori,

I give up. I have no brother and no best friend. Don't have Andrew either, but whatever.

They're all gone. And I think it's my fault. Something's wrong with me. I've always had unhappy thoughts about them before they died. Do I have mind powers or something?

Mom doesn't believe it's my fault.

I don't want to go to school tomorrow. Maybe I'll bring you with me. You seem to be my only friend—a friend that never leaves me.

— Katie

Friday, May 13

Dear Dori,

Mom let me stay home. I told her I didn't want to go to school. I felt too crappy to take even one step out of the house. I locked myself in my room, and here I am, talking to you. I have Billy's DS on and sitting next to me. He's finally beating Princess Peach in a race. And Lauren gave up running around her music. She's sitting on the treble clef, swinging her legs. I wonder what Andrew is doing?

I decided it's my fault. I told you that though, didn't I? Maybe you could help me? I don't know what to do. I just want it all to stop.

Haha, my brother's happy. He's jumping up and down right now, rubbing it in. Peach doesn't look too happy, which is weird. Isn't she always smiling? It's always a happy ending for Peach. Haha, Wario's happy for Billy. Billy always played Wario. Funny how they end up being best of friends. Like me and Lauren were…

Lauren and I seem to have made up for our fight. It's all my fault, and it was hard getting the point across. She can't hear me talk, so I was pretty much acting out what I was trying to say. We both ended up laughing, and now we're friends again as if we never fought in the first place.

I want to play my flute, but I'm afraid to. Maybe if I just don't think of anyone, it'll be alright. Yeah, maybe I'll do that. I'll talk to you in a few.

— Katie

I set my purple diary aside and picked up my flute case from the floor. In due time, music was scattered across my bed, and my flute felt cool beneath my hands. The open-hole keys were covered with my fingertips, and I started playing my solo—the solo that killed Billy.

I couldn't get into it at the thought of Billy. I put my flute down, reached for Dori, and started writing.

No, I'll try again, I thought. Putting aside my diary, I reached for band music and practiced my solo. I could hear Mr. Trace telling me to follow the dynamics because what I played was so flat and boring. I shoved that music aside and resorted to playing "Mary Had A Little Lamb".

I hated myself.

My body kept playing, but my mind wandered again. I was a horrible person. I couldn't get along with Billy; I insulted Andrew way too many times, considering all the times he was kind to me; and I overreacted and fought with Lauren, who was only trying to help me. I wished I go back in time and try this all again. Maybe things would turn out for the better.

But there was no such thing as time travel, and I resumed hating myself. There was nothing to do. I killed three people somehow, and no one would forgive me. I'm a murderer deserving Death Row, to be executed, to be sent away and secluded from all of society.

However, if I was sent to prison, I would learn to hate the police; and they would drop dead. I was a hopeless cause. I was good for nothing.

I loved music. I always have, and I always would. For one reason, Dori…

"Katie, open up," Julie said again, knocking on her daughter's bedroom door. "We need to talk. Lauren's mother called. Katie, open the door."

Julie sighed and walked to her room. She returned with a key and unlocked the door.

"Katie?" Julie walked over to the bed and shook her daughter. "Katie? Are you asleep?" It was odd how Katie wasn't waking up. She was always a light sleeper. "Oh, my gosh…" Julie felt for Katie's pulse, and her eyes bulged. "Oh, my gosh, Katie! Katie! No, Katie! Oh, my gosh!" Julie sobbed into her daughter's shirt, hugging Katie tightly. "Don't leave me too. Please, don't go. I love you, Katie. Please…"

Katie's flute laid innocently on the bed, glittering in the sun's light. It was a beautiful flute, and it was even more gorgeous with Katie playing it. No one Julie knew could play better than Katie, even Lauren. Katie was Julie's star, and the flute shone as if it were the reason Katie was so great. Julie could almost see its personality; it's cocky character as if it were better than anyone else; as if it *knew* what happened to all those people and laughed at Julie. *Laughed.*

Still sobbing, her eyes landed on Katie's opened diary, sitting right in front of Katie as if she was writing in it before…

She laid Katie in a comfortable position, and picked up the purple book. Julia opened it to the last page, and dropped it, crying into her daughter's shoulder once again.

Dear Dori,

It's not just black notes.

It's a whole different language.

AUTUMN KISSED

Sophie W.

19 (F) of New York, USA

When furled leaves glide on blue sky wings, and land
In whispering, watercolored heaps; when sharp
The tongues of frosty air that lick the grass
To ashen gray; when in the sighing breaths
Of wind the maple waves its bony arms;
I shuffle, brown and shriveled, to this place.

Where once we wandered in the quiet light--
Your freckled face, these same soft hands--and kissed
Beneath this lasting tree, its silver bark
Still smooth--I stand now looking back through years
Of sliding seasons, changing dreams, and reach
For slipping memory of tender days.

And though the crumbled leaves form dust that flies
Far from your grave, and apple cider spills
From lips too old to kiss your face, the fall
Still comes, before the lonely winter months,
And sweeps us close once more. So underneath

A clear blue sky, while love-red leaves drift down,

And walnut shells, a poison-green, begin

To split, the echoes soft float through the air

Of laughter here: we're autumn kissed again.

BURNT SAUSAGES
Mark C.

16 (M) of Worcestershire, England

'Why is Daddy making us sleep under the grill?'

He is curled next to Marie, who sits on the desert with her two legs crossed like a game of Noughts and Crosses.

She's silent.

She's as silent as the cruel Sun overhead, a gloating candle, piercing the rough blanket of ash that spreads from the wreckage, the last protection against his burning light.

'Why is Daddy snoring so quietly?'

Again, Mummy doesn't answer. Mummy's angry with her. Mummy just drops her head forward and stares at the sand with two tea light eyes. Like everyone else. Everyone glares at the ground, with red paint licking their bodies. They have no use for words, hoping instead to penetrate the sand in the same way Daddy does to Marie when she's naughty.

Heat shivers her body. She embraces Mummy like she embraces Teddy, but does not cry, because Daddy always tells her that she must be grateful.

She hugs her tighter. Because Mummy's cold, cold like the water at the seaside. But the sand she sits on now is nothing like the sand at the shore. This sand is rough, hot; sprinkles of sugar on the ground, not tasting like sugar at all, but a sour lemon, one with no flavour and that Daddy stole from her favourite tree before it yellowed.

Someone has taken the blue from the sea and thrown it into the sky, leaving big cracks and potholes all across the desert which stare at Marie, luring her over.

'Sorry, I need to get home. I'll ask Daddy if I am allowed to stay out, but he'll say no.'

The eyebrows of the drifting heat waver up and down in agreement, wobbling the horizon.

With the smiling face of a puppy, she lifts her face to greet the brushing warmth, in which she cowers to Daddy in a face that only Sweetheart could.

'Can I go and play with the sand?'

Silent.

She has enflamed him.

She doesn't want *that* at all.

Yes, Sweetheart.

She bounds up and skips away. After a few moments, she looks back, watching all the colours of fire burn above the sand. She wants some marshmallows to roast and chew quickly, but elects to not ask angry Daddy. Perhaps he can sense the guilt upon his chest. Mummy and Daddy have always said *not to play with your toys like that!* because they break, and Daddy has broken this plane.

It's bitter.

The taste of black ash in the air is bitter. And she smells the Earth. She smells nobody's footsteps. Because it's beyond reproach; it's untouched like Marie's bedroom that Mummy hates. But there is the smell of burning meat, food—burnt sausages, yes. And it's coming from inside the plane where the people sit in their seats in complete tranquillity.

Fires rage around them.

Deafening.

She looks back to the sky, where the grey cigarette smoke, like Daddy's, is no longer floating. The Sun is holding back the sea. And there she dances, on the seabed of a cracked earth, singing the lullaby that Seaside Nanny used to sing to her.

Water, water everywhere… not a drop to spare.

How does the rhyme finish? She forgets. She asks the desert. He can't remember either, so she wonders atop her new playing field with her new friends.

Water, water everywhere… Marie does not care.

That's stupid, Marie, stupid! The Sun shakes her head and uses the captive water as poison, visions telling her that the sea wants to come home, back down onto the seabed where the laces of the Earth's hair flourish as seaweed. Breaking in a few diamonds, tears begin to flow down her cheeks. She's sorry. She tells that to the Sun.

Her lips are crusty, like the edges of bread. She has always hated the crust of bread. But Daddy says that it's good for her, so then, she asks, 'Why drink water if it gets rid of the crust on your lips?'

Then, he pretends to ignore her.

And lifts his hand as if to stroke her hair.

He does.

A moment of silence waves as it passes by on a train into the indefinite skyline.

Then he gives her a nosebleed.

I'm so thirsty.

* * *

The second of potential—flames leap from the bonfire and tear the heavens apart as thunder, sending God his wakeup call. Marie suspects that He's still in slumber; He's letting Mummy and Daddy burn.

But something tells her that Mummy and Daddy aren't there at all. They are with Him. And Marie sees what the Sun is waiting for.

Her.

She slips forward, and hits the crack of the desert.

Gone from her silhouette, she closes her eyes. And blinks. She's awake again.

In the crystal blue heaven.

The sea of souls.

LOVE'S LAST WISH
Heather E.

12 (F) of Washington, USA

My nameless beauty,
so polite, so strong.
Some wish her grief,

but I wish her love.
I tell her to tell me her wish—
I shall grant it.
She whispers in my ear all that she can say,
"I wish we never meet again."

Although my heart weeps,
her wish is not of hate
but of love.
Bound by my promise,
I must grant the wish,
So I do,

and slowly walk away from her death bed.

WORDS
Mairi T.

18 (F) of Aberdeenshire, Scotland

Even for late evening, even for late in the year these hours were dark. As the sky turned to ink by degrees, the light inside came closer to cruel. The streetlamps smouldered in the alleyway beyond, but it was the clinical glow in the kitchen which brought out the charcoal circles beneath Chris' eyes. And so he found himself framed by the square window, aching with every move Wren made in the next room.

It wasn't the house which had him haggard. After so many weeks of sharing it, this was even starting to feel like home. His little sister's place was small enough to feel cramped when filled with three adults and her Labrador, and that the cardboard boxes which lined the walls in abundance were beginning to dent at the corners. Wren in particular was adept at stubbing her toe on the way past. Somehow, though, the extra bodies brightened the place more kindly than the overhead lighting did now.

The door to the living room was open, and the television muttered to herald in the late news. He sighed, filled the kettle and threw it on the hob.

Increasingly, of evenings, he was aware of his heart. He had even been known to count its beating in his ears. It was a kinder way of passing the minutes than letting his thoughts run away.

Chris' eyes settled on the calendar Wren had pinned, in between a glorious three year's worth of postcards, to the corkboard. She had had fun with it, he noticed, not for the first time. She had had fun to such an extent that, in their younger days, he might have turned his nose up. There were balloons doodled next to birthdays, with highlighters. There were sad faces beside the numerous dentist appointments required of wisdom teeth, or days to pay rent. There were tiny roses in the corners of anniversary days...

"Turn it down," he finally snapped.

Even from the next room, Wren could tell it was a plea rather than the order he made it seem. Chris' words had broken in the middle so, lightly, she obliged. She had learned by now not to ask questions when it came to the news.

He came to join her in another minute. Wren moved one of the boxes from the sofa to let him sit, then settled back down. She had work to do, deadlines to meet, and as soon as the box was balanced on the armrest, they fell into routine silence. She sat comfortably, legs crossed on the cushion with a bundle of children's jotters in her lap. They were brightly coloured, like a stack of Christmas gifts, and she smiled occasionally at the stories they had written for her. *When I Grow Up, I Want To Be...* The encouragement and gentle guidance flowed from her pen in green ink. As her wrist twitched, her bracelet threw off little rings of light.

But gradually, irresistibly, her gaze fell to a threadbare patch on the carpet. Chris continued to stare at the television, his gaze so intent he seemed now to be trying to lip read. Some offensive report about the war was drawing to a close. From the corner of her eye, Wren saw him shiver.

"It sounds worse out there," she at last observed.

"When has it ever been good news?"

She smiled weakly and tossed him the remote. Chris lowered the volume further, though the advert break was harmless enough. Even then he glowered at the set with enough vehemence to melt the news reader who had long since vacated the screen. To read, detached, from an autocue the names of some he had known as part of a death register was inexcusable.

They had mentioned duty in the official statement, as he knew already. That morning, he had gleaned it from the newspaper while no one was looking and then tossed the whole thing into the recycling box before he had been disturbed. Destruction of inescapable truths was his duty to them, this house, or more accurately, to Katherine.

The news returned. The opening screen was slightly less dramatic now that the fanfare was mute.

Wren sighed. She tried to stretch out to counteract the stiffness that her brother's mood had brought to the living room, but to little effect. In the process of raising her arms she even managed to dent another box with her elbow. These new hazards were only for another few weeks, she reminded herself, not necessarily with relief. Chris' things, Katherine's things, their things would leave along with them as soon as their shiny new key was bestowed. If Chris was looking forward to that moment, he didn't show it now. In spite of everything, his foul humour had overtaken him.

It wasn't as if she could blame him. To be a soldier, as Chris still was, at a time like this? It was something of a nightmare. Her face had drained completely at the thought.

"Kate's scared for you." At last, from nowhere, Wren looked up. "She won't even read the newspapers."

"Can you talk about something else?"

"I mean," she stuttered on, "you can't blame her. The numbers are pretty horrifying."

"Wren." The way he spoke her name was sharp, despite that familiar, young beseech in his eyes. His gaze caught and lingered like a threat. "Please."

They had the same eyes, their mother's, a blue closer to denim jeans than to the poster paint of the children's drawings in the kitchen. It seemed strange to Wren that she could barely even recognise him.

Katherine's eyes were brightest green.

Even to remember them set a weight of panic on his chest. Chris had seen her twenty minutes ago, happy, yet all he could think about were the tears he was going to bring to her. As they rose, they would be water trying to glaze over rock, to re-establish calm, to beg. He had been away from home since she had loved him, but not in a climate like this, not with the start of a life to leave behind.

His soldier's heart had been forged for him long before the heat of the desert could cause it to shatter. Katherine had melted it again with one glimpse of her beautiful face, her satin laugh, her hands, the light in her eyes. The only mark of the soldier's heart still on him was the irresistible compulsion of that word "duty."

"Your flat should be ready soon," Wren commented. She dropped her work to the floor. *When I Grow Up, I Want To Be an Army Man...* had been a little too much.

"Just another fortnight. Three weeks at the most."

He rubbed at his neck, trying to order his thoughts, trying to order anything. Wren might as well have been flicking her feeble words off the marble arm of a statue.

"Are you excited yet?"

"Kate is," he admitted. Her name snagged in his throat more roughly than before. "But then, she still has a wedding to plan."

From the kitchen, the kettle started to rumble gently. The darkness in the corners of the room became pronounced. It seeped from between boxes and into the hollows of his face. Her lips pursed.

"You haven't set a date yet, have you?"

Chris' head belonged in his hands, but he settled on shaking it slowly.

"You should. She's always struck me as the kind for a summer wedding, you know. The pictures on a lawn somewhere in the sun, the cherry trees out in the background. If you don't do it soon, she'll have to wait another eighteen months."

"They're sending me back."

Sickly enough, he smiled. If only at the way the words sounded let loose, unbridled, indefatigable, blunt. He watched her reel. Even with her happy face, the front of optimism which came from life as a primary teacher, he had struck her down. It was the same way his parents would reel, the same way a choice few friends had reeled already. Perhaps it was a shadow of the axe blow it would be to Kate.

Wren sighed at last. "It's hardly unexpected."

He was quick to tell her that that didn't make it right.

"Have you told her?"

The kettle rumbled louder. Chris moved into the kitchen to find some coffee mugs, or to retreat, Wren couldn't quite judge. She turned in her seat to keep watching him which, childlike, he pretended not to notice.

"Chris?"

He moved as though each muscle ached.

How long ago had he seen this coming? It was watching the car tear towards his unprotected form, the headlights blinding, too appalled to step from its path, too horror struck even to dive in front of her. Wren was right, this was always going to happen. But Kate had forgotten and he had lived. They had moved on together and suddenly there was meaning in the day. The truth of it all was raw in his mind, yet he spoke at the same moment his name left her lips.

"I am terrified that something is going to happen and I won't be here when she needs me. I won't be able to protect her." His words went into the high cupboard, since he refused to turn around. It wasn't enough to let his voice to pass as level. He had even put his fist against the wall.

"How can I save her from my funeral?"

He thought of his last months on the battlegrounds. Out there, with luck, he might be a brother to those men around him, but he shouldn't have had a life over which to grow homesick. He certainly wasn't a fiancé. Out there, there was no new house, no afternoons of dog sitting for his sister. The world, the game was the grey of the city streets and the barren waste beyond their borders. The heat, the hate, the dust, the noise, the earth ploughed and corrugated with the burrows of innumerable shells. Two friends lost in three weeks. A photograph of Katherine with the light of a sunset soft on the line of her cheek left dog-eared and water damaged, the subtlety of her smile worn away in an operation lasting only six weeks. That had been before the conflict had escalated.

Of silence and stating the obvious, Wren was choosing the kinder option. The latter didn't go unexpressed, of course. The latter was keeping Chris awake into the small hours, because the truth was that this had been his choice. He had enlisted. He had volunteered. Willingly, he had led both of them into the uncertainties of this life. He just hadn't signed on for nights like this.

He set the mugs down hard on the worktop.

"I tried to write her a letter."

She knew what he meant. *The* letter. The one he had once, jokingly, asked if she would hold onto in case the very worst should happen. Hollywood attempts to say the things for which there were no words at all. She winced, but only inside.

"The ring wasn't enough?"

He couldn't suppress a grin. She had said yes. That was still enough for his heartbeat to make itself known.

He threw the teabags into the mugs and went to the fridge.   "I failed anyway. I tried for hours to get something down and all I ended up with was writer's cramp."

"What did you say?"

Chris shook his head again. Living together, closer than they had ever been as children, she still didn't get to know everything.

But he had told her everything over two dozen redrafts, a whole ream of good paper. Assurances of love, contemplations of another life, dirges for the future they were meant for. They had sounded brittle, false even, without the chance to look into her eyes. It wasn't as if he could end the letter either, sign his name with a flourish and then seal the envelope with a precious kiss. In his head, every word which jarred from his pen had taken on a double meaning, every clause of every run on sentence was brackish even now. He would pin down the feeling, and it would run from his grasp, leaving its less articulate cousin to tumble out in permanent ink to hurt her more. Most consistently of all, though, he had told her to hate him, and to rest assured that he was hating himself.

"Did you mean it?" Wren had to ask. "That's all that matters."

"I meant every single, clumsy, inarticulate word. That doesn't mean she deserves it." His fist was balled. The steam rose from the kettle beside him. The steel lid rattled. "That's not even the worst part."

Chris laughed, cutting her off as she tried to tell him that he simply hadn't found the right words. It was an arid kind of a laugh, a bark. Words could topple empires, but his were all inadequate. He didn't want to leave her with a handwriting sample. Even if she read it until she knew the words by heart and the paper fell apart at the creases it would be nothing. All the words in the world weren't enough. All the words in the world were bullets.

The kettle boiled. It whistled so shrilly that it cut through every knot and tangle in the house. Chris snatched it from the hob, knocking over the mugs in the process.

His fell to the floor and shattered. Five pieces of the rim flew to different edges of the room. Each half of the handle settled at the corner of a different cardboard box. Wren stood up smoothly and went to pick up the pieces as her brother went quiet again. Chris staggered to the other counter, shaking his head, staring at the annotated calendar. His mouth was open. His hands raked through his hair.

"I leave in a week."

Wren was silenced.

The shards of pottery cut into her skin as she tried to pinpoint the call which had come, the news, the day when things had changed. He looked to be grieving, so how was it that she hadn't noticed? The anger rose before the tears had the chance to. Now she knew what it was to reel.

Hands shaking, she placed the largest fragment on the tabletop.

"When did they tell you?"

"I don't remember. A month?" he smiled wryly. "I just haven't been able to admit it to myself." Then, darkest of all. "She's never going to forgive me."

When she was angry, you could see Wren's occupation. Her fingers were still steady as they scraped through her hair, but he could see in her eyes that she wanted to look down on him. Her thin hands wrung together. Her nails left little half moon scores in her palms. Chris understood, of course. Her anger, his lack of planning, all of it brought the battlefront to their home. Quite apart from that, to let days decrease exponentially and still sleep beside Katherine was selfishness the like of which he didn't understand himself.

Concentrating on breathing, Wren faced the reassurance because really, her feelings on the matter were worth nothing.

"She understands," she breathed at last.

"Everything I say is going to hurt her more."

"She understands."

Chris' voice had cracked as it rose. Wren's was a shattered whisper at the rhythm of Katherine's bare feet on the stairs.

The door pushed back. The children's drawings fluttered.

"Understand what?" she asked, her face still full of light despite the hour. Her voice was like a climbing rose.

The mug breaking, she had come to investigate. Kate smiled more genuinely than the other two, hugging a dressing gown around her slight frame. Always willowy, she now looked fragile beneath it.

Something in her eyes went out as the sheer weight in their faces registered.

"Understand what?"

Chris stared helplessly between her face and the clock, only to see the future, to see his choke weed words, lying there forever beside her broken soul. The second hand took longer than it should have to move. The stone was cast. Everything was about to break. The clock, with the oversized numbers at every quarter hour, ticked loudly enough to be heard in their silence. The house kept words of its own.

ABOUT SOMETHING
Siiri T.

17 (F) of Kirkkonummi, Finland

If you want to tell me
about something beautiful,
tell me about a rose ribbon

in the morning sky,
tell me about a snowy forest
beneath the stars:
tell me about silence.

If you want to tell me
about something pleasant,
tell me about woollen socks
with colourful stripes,
tell me about hot chocolate
with whipped cream –
tell me about yourself.

If you want to tell me
about something secret,

tell me about the relaxing song
of April raindrops,
or about the running thought
of an animator.
Tell me about prejudice.

And when you finally give me
the chance to talk,
I'll tell you how
I already know such things.
I'll tell you about
you being unable to awe me –
I listened without learning anything new.

CHROMATOGRAPHY

Baqiyyah H.

16 (F) of New York, USA

"Mother, what makes the sky blue?"

She is sitting, drawing on a sheet of pink construction paper. Her chubby fist grips the brown crayon, her chin resting on her left hand.

"It was created blue," Mother says from the rocking chair besides the sunny window, and turns back to her sewing.

The girl returns to her picture. Dark, heavy strokes of blue march across the top of the page, perpendicular to the thick, vertical line of brown.

"Mother, why is the grass green?"

"From the sun."

She drags the crayon across the page again, and then tosses it back amongst the others.

"But the sun is yellow, mother."

"Mm hm." Mother rocks back and forth, her hands moving swiftly with her needlework.

"Then if the sun is yellow, why is the grass green?"

Her hand hovers over the bin of crayons and picks up a thin, yellow one. She reaches for a fresh sheet of paper, and slides a white one from the pile. She draws a circle in the top right corner, filling it in heavily. The crayon begins to bend under the pressure.

"Mother, you know why I chose a skinny one?"

"I don't know, dear," Mother says, "tell me."

"Because, the sticks of light that the sun grows are very skinny. A fat crayon couldn't make them." She shakes her head for emphasis.

She seizes the blue crayon again and repeats the deep marks across the top of the page. The blue overlaps the long, yellow rays of the sun, turning the spots green.

"Mother, why is the sun yellow if the sky is blue?"

"Because they were created differently, just like me and you."

She nods without questioning and continues to scribble, the colors reaching the middle of the page.

She picks up a black crayon and draws shapes like lowercase M's across the dark blue field.

"These are birds, Mother. They're black, like crows." Mother's chair creaks as it rocks. "I would draw seagulls and swans and pelicans, but the white crayon doesn't work."

She reaches for green, and draws short tick-marks at the bottom of the page. She pauses, peeling the paper away from the dull point of the crayon.

"Mother," she squeals excitedly, "I know why the grass is green!"

Mother looks up and smiles, "Why, dear?"

"Because," the girl explains, her small body shaking with excitement, "the sky is blue, and the sun is yellow. Yellow and blue makes green."

"Yes, dear," Mother says, not completely understanding.

"So when the yellow comes down through the blue sky, it sprinkles green all over!"

SHATTERED
Heather M.

16 (F) of Co. Antrim, Northern Ireland

Shattered like the piece of broken glass
I accidentally smashed on the wooden floor.
Shattered like the pieces of my heart,
When you say you won't see me anymore.

Was it something I did that hurt you,
Or just something stupid I've said?
I can't seem to shake these feelings;
The scattered thoughts in my head.

Tell me if I've done something wrong
Can't we both just try to pretend?
Tell me, when did you change your mind?
I thought we'd be together until the end.

So as you take off your golden ring,
And set it on the wooden table;
As you break the promise of forever,
I try to speak but I find I'm unable.

You softly whisper, 'I'm sorry'
And I fall crumbling to the ground.
You clean up the pile of shattered glass,
And then disappear without a sound.

THE THWARTED ATTEMPT AT SHOWERING IN STONES
Yehuda C.

18 (M) of Johannesburg, South Africa

The elephantine structure loomed overhead. It was the first of its kind to reach completion, and from the ground it appeared to be a gigantic scarlet spiraled balloon, somehow hovering in mid-air. But it was far more then that. It was a skyscraper like none other before it. It was tall, yes, but no taller than many other buildings in the vicinity. This skyscraper was unique because it was the first building in the world to float above the ground. Marriott International had begun the project eight years before, likely in the hope that it would put all of its rivals to shame. They claimed, though, that its intent was to revive the dying economy of Manhattan. After all, eco-tourism was the only sector that kept Manhattan's economy even moderately alive, and a flying hotel would certainly do wonders for it.

The Flying Marriott, as had become the name of the hotel chain's newest project, relied on a technology far beyond any the world had experienced, and was, theoretically at least, as firmly planted in the air as any building could be on land. It boasted incomparable luxuries, and promised remarkable sights, the likes of which could not be seen anywhere else in the world. Least of these was Central Park, which was visible from the Hotel in its entirety. Along with the rest of Manhattan, Central Park had deteriorated. Prior to this historic event, it was decrepit, and in desperate need of renovation, but for the grand opening of The Flying Marriott, Marriott International had given it one. The park was restored to its former days of glory, and this New Year's Eve had been marked as it's reincarnation.

It would begin only at midnight, yet the park had an intense atmosphere already, seven hours before the monumental event. The winter evening was freezing cold, yet this had not deterred the droves of people who had turned out to become a part of history. The park contained an indiscriminate array of people that night. Young, old, rich and poor people had all gathered from around the world to New York to witness the fireworks display that would outshine any other, and had already several days before the event, been hailed as the greatest of all time. Every person in the park would watch the fireworks, but few would play any role other than spectator. There were the hundreds of policemen who had been hired to control the crowd if things got out of hand, there were the firemen who had been hired to ensure that no stray firecracker would cause lasting damage, and there were the rare individuals whose job it was to change the course of history.

On an old rickety bench that decorated the edge of a path with an almost vintage feel, a wholly unremarkable person sat. Or so it seemed. He never revealed his true name, but instead chose to walk around under an alias: Kenneth Samuels. The name was not a memorable one, nor was it too common, for, Kenneth Samuels' job description required him to remain as forgettable as a person could. When working for an intelligence agency, it is expected that one blends into his surroundings avoiding all attention, a task at which Kenneth was perfectly adept. He glanced at his wristwatch. Ten after five. The setting sun indicated that the afternoon was drawing to a close. He opened a rugged briefcase, replaced the New York Times that he had been reading, and rose with a tired grimace as he began to make his way across the park to Central Park West.

A half hour later, Kenneth strode through the revolving door that marked the entrance to an apartment building, nodding briefly to the doorman as he passed. He ran up seven flights of stairs, grabbed the tuxedo that hung on his doorknob, and hurried inside. He did not want to draw attention to himself by arriving late to The Flying Marriott's opening party.

"You're five minutes late," a voice from the living room called.

"Sorry dear," he said, "The streets were more crowded than I've ever seen them."

"It's fine, but you'll need to get ready pretty fast, they expect us to arrive at eight o'clock sharp, so we'll need to leave here at six-thirty," his wife said. "That gives you just under an hour to get all decked out."

"I know, Stephie," he replied blandly, "I'll get straight to the shower."

At ten minutes past six, Kenneth Samuels emerged from the dressing room in a freshly pressed, black tuxedo. His dark hair sat neatly gelled behind his ears, and his usually short stubble had been shaved off. His wife gave him a small kiss, and took hold of his hand with the smell of an expensive aftershave lingering in the air.

"Let's go," Stephanie said, "it can't hurt to arrive a few minutes early. It might give you a little more time to get to know the terrain."

"Let's just stay another five minutes."
"Okay dear," Stephanie said, "but only five minutes." She slumped into his lap and put her head on his chest.

"Stephanie," Kenneth said.

"Yes dear?" Stephanie replied.

"After we have conducted the necessary formalities, I want you to take the shuttle down to the ground. When you are down, take an uptown 1 train to 239th street. It's not safe, I know, but trust me, it's safer than it is in Manhattan. Well, at least for tonight. Can you do this?" He looked desperate, as he watched her expression grow... almost tired.

"What makes this mission so much more dangerous than usual?" asked Stephanie.

"Look Stephanie, you know I'm not allowed to give you any inside information, but tonight, as you know, a hotel will be opening in the sky. Directly above Central Park in fact. Thousands of people will be in the park, and hundreds more in the hotel. If you wanted to sabotage the event, what would you do?"

Stephanie's face paled. "You're telling me that someone's going to try to knock the hotel out of the sky?" she asked incredulously. "And what would anyone gain from doing such a thing?"

"Sorry Stephanie, but you know I can't tell you," Kenneth said. He paused briefly. "So what's it going to be? Will you do as I ask?"

"What if I say no?"

"Then I will be forced to go about the mission in the fear that you might die." He looked into her eyes, "I couldn't stand that." A long silence followed. "I intend to crash their party at ten minutes to eleven. If anything goes wrong, you'll need to be out of the city by then."

The limousine pulled up at the entrance to The Sky Marriott. It was by no means the only limousine on the block. In fact, those who had not arrived in limousines, had arrived in Ferraris, Porsches, or other equally impressive cars. The shuttle would leave from a small building very elaborately adorned with marble floors and what appeared to be a gold door frame. Kenneth opened the door with Stephanie at his arm. The room was filled with guards who donned blue uniforms, and x-ray machines reminiscent of an airport terminal.

"Tickets," a guard said curtly.

Kenneth opened his wallet, and handed the guard Stephanie's ticket together with his own.

"These appear to be in order. Remove your shoes and your belt,Sir, Ma'am. Then move on to the next counter, and place all electronic equipment separately into the x-ray machine," The guard paused as if for effect. "And you will need to hand in any weapons you are carrying."

The shuttle that appeared after the security check looked remarkably like an elevator. A security guard led them into the shuttle whose walls were made of a thick glass, but the roof and floor seemed to be made of a silver aluminum. Inside it, a man and a woman, who were presumably a couple stood waiting.

"Kenneth Samuels," a friendly voice came from his side, "How lovely it is to see you once again. And this must be your wife?" The man didn't wait for a response before he offered Stephanie his hand. "Gordon Fredricks, a pleasure to meet you." Gordon didn't look remotely interested.

She took his hand unenthusiastically. "Stephanie Samuels."

The other woman glared at Gordon.

"Oh, how rude of me," Gordon said, "I haven't introduced my escort, this is Candice. Candice, this is Kenneth Samuels, and his wife Stephanie," he introduced the two as though Candice had not heard him greet them. An awkward silence followed.

A thick metal rope passed through each of the four corners. The shuttle slowly ascended as the metal ropes seemed to spiral through the floor. It wasn't too long before a view of the southern part of the park came into view over the row of buildings that hid the shuttle from Central Park South. Lights of greens, blues and reds flashed in all directions. Thousands of people were visible in the park below scattered over the park's magnificent white cover of snow. As the shuttle rose higher, trees that were covered with a white frost frost emerged among the lights, and a light flurry decorated the air. The shuttle's four occupants stared transfixed down at the magnificent park beneath them. The sight was breathtaking.

The ride up to the hotel lasted five short minutes. The shuttle door opened, and Kenneth reluctantly followed the guard through the door. Stephanie squeezed his hand tightly. They were by no means the earliest, in fact many people had already arrived, and were sipping cocktails. The room was massive. Two staircases ascended to a second floor, and they then sunk into the ground, leading to a basement of sorts.

"Oh, I'm sorry, Kenneth, but I've just seen someone I need to talk to," Gordon said almost as soon as they had exited the shuttle. "Excuse us." with that, he walked over to the side of an extremely tall man dragging Candice behind him.

"How do you know that guy, Ken?" asked Stephanie as soon as he was out of earshot.

"Oh, you mean old Gordon? He's well known in business circles," said Kenneth. "He's filthy rich, but gives a lot to charity, mind you. Made a mint with his garbage incineration scheme. He's retired now, and is only forty. He's a bit of a nerd really."

An hour later, after most of the social requirements had been fulfilled, the crowd began to move downstairs for dinner.

"Excuse me, Stephanie," said Kenneth, "I need to go to the restrooms. Please wait here for me until I return."

"Of course, dear."

Kenneth moved forward apparently following the signs which indicated the restrooms. But after studying the plans of the hotel for several days, he knew perfectly well where they were, and no signs were necessary to guide him there. There were several others using the restrooms, but fortunately the middle cubicle was vacant. He entered it, and locked the door behind him. He looked down into the bowl, and wrinkled his nose. He silently lifted the lid of the tank off revealing the two Glock 22 pistols that were taped to it. He removed them, and tucked one into the back of his belt. He slipped the other one in his pants pocket, in the hope that its shape would be hidden by his tuxedo. He replaced the tank's lid, and left the cubicle. A man at the basins paused his hand-washing to give him a disgusted look and it was only it was only after a few seconds, that Kenneth realized, and with a quick apology reentered the cubicle, and flushed the toilet before he left.

Stephanie waited for him next to the stairway that would lead down to the banquet hall. He took her hand as they walked into the banquet hall. The center of the hall was left open, with at least fifty tables surrounding it. The band played a slow bluesy ballad.

"Do you want to dance?" he asked.

"Okay," Stephanie smiled. Kenneth led her to the dance floor. Halfway there Stephanie gasped. It didn't take long for him to work out what it was that had blown her away. The dance floor was made entirely of glass. And directly beneath them, the lights of Central Park flashed.

Kenneth led Stephanie across the dance floor in a slow waltz. She put her head against his chest. After a few silent paces, Kenneth leaned closer to her ear.

"Put your hand at the base of my back, and take the gun out of my belt," he whispered.

"What? I thought you weren't involving me in this," Stephanie replied – just as softly.

"It's not for now, it's in case someone starts up with you uptown." She hesitated, but then he felt her ease the weapon out of his belt strap. "Good, now as we make this next turn, pass it into my left hand. I'm going to tuck it underneath that shoulder strap. Your scarf should hide it adequately."

"When are you going to get moving?" she asked.

"Let's dance a little longer," he said. "I'll leave after dinner. That'll give me two hours until midnight, and forty five or so minutes before I play my part."

"I'll leave at the same time then. A half hour is enough to get out of Manhattan," Stephanie said. "We can separate in the entrance hall."

Dinner was served at a prompt nine-thirty. The menu comprised of a choice of roast duck with raspberry glaze, filet mignon, and an option of a vegetable tempura for vegetarians. A rich scent of Middle-Eastern spices permeated the air as the food arrived at the table. Conversation ceased almost immediately, as the room suddenly became engrossed in its food. Kenneth raised his knife and cut through his steak, revealing a rare, red inside. Stephanie winced, looked away, and prodded her vegetable tempura.

"If you have to eat an animal," Stephanie said, "can't you at least cook it?"

"No, it's more juicy this way," Kenneth responded unconcerned.

"Are you also a vegetarian?" Stephanie looked across the table. It was Dorian Campbell who had asked the question. He was the successful entrepreneur who had started Campbell Enterprises, one of the leading security system developers in the world. Stephanie nodded as they both cringed as Kenneth sliced another piece of meat.

Ten o'clock arrived before Kenneth and Stephanie politely excused themselves from the table. Kenneth left his tuxedo jacket on the back of the his seat, and with his tie flapping, and Stephanie at his arm, he exited the banquet hall. After bidding Stephanie a brief goodbye, Kenneth did not wait for her to leave the hall before he moved up the stairway that would, after thirty floors take him to the roof's deck. After the first level, the stairway would be accessed through a door. If he *was* expected, he would be expected to arrive in the elevator.

The stairway was fairly steep, and was illuminated only by the electric torches on its walls intended to give it a medieval feel, which, Kenneth could not help but notice, was sorely lacking in quality. It felt more like New York did in one of its frequent blackouts. The stairs disappeared under his feet as he ascended. The fireworks display would be launched from the upper deck, which was in fact the roof of the hotel. If the terrorists had there way, though, the fireworks display would last far shorter than was anticipated. All the fireworks launched together in a strategic location had the energy needed to topple The Sky Marriott on to the million or so people in Central Park. They did not need to bring explosives into the hotel – the explosives were already there.

The sign at the door leading out to the suites indicated that Kenneth had arrived at the fortieth floor. The deck would be accessed through a telephone booth-like structure with an opaque wooden covering to hide the stairway. This would provide the cover necessary for his attack, giving him the vital element of surprise. Unfortunately, he had instructions to only detain Achmed Zarawani. The agency needed him *alive*, meaning that he couldn't just barge in and shoot whoever he saw. No, this would require a certain skill possessed by few, not to mention the careful hours of planning that had gone into it.

Silently, Kenneth Samuels ascended to the final level. With each step his heart seemed to beat faster. The final few steps seemed to take the longest to climb. He could hear the silence of the staircase interrupted now by an urgent chatter in a foreign dialect that he recognized as Farsi. After spending four years in Iran, he could understand it fluently.

"Come, get into position," Kenneth heard a man's voice say.

"What happens if he arrives early?" He didn't know if the men were talking about him, but that was exactly what he intended to do, and at precisely ten-twenty one, he loaded his gun, and kicked the door open. The six men on the roof jumped in alarm, and the room erupted into chaos.

Kenneth immediately spotted Zarawani, and positioned his arm accordingly in order to avoid shooting him. He intended to take advantage of the confusion he had created, and before any of the terrorists could blink an eye, Kenneth had fired three shots, each burying itself into the terrorists' skulls. Three down, three to go.

By this time, one of the remaining three had managed to produce a Russian crafted AK-74 assault rifle. Kenneth ignored the other two, and ran at him kneeing him in the groin before he managed to lift the weapon. He keeled over, and Kenneth shot him twice in the head.

Two were left. Zarawani and the other remaining terrorist had apparently both found weapons. Both of which were pointing at him. Time froze; he would only be able to kill one of them. And even if he disobeyed orders and killed Zarawani, as long as there was one terrorist alive, the plot would succeed. One terrorist was enough to ignite all the fireworks together, and knock The Flying Marriott out of the sky, and kill all of those civilians in Central Park as well. Thousands would die, and he would have saved nobody.

The time had come. He fired a single shot at Zarawani's companion, pulling the trigger, and diving sideways simultaneously. Several bullets whizzed over his head. Zarawani's companion dropped down dead. Kenneth pushed himself up, and lifted his head as he surveyed the deck for Zarawani.

"I'm right here, Mr Samuels" a voice said from beside him in an only lightly accented English. The barrel of a rifle was pressed painfully into his back.

"Zarawani," he seethed. He knew he didn't dare turn around.

"Why don't you put down your gun? And remember, one sudden movement, and I pull the trigger." the terrorist said. Kenneth slowly lowered his gun to the floor. "I'm impressed Mr Samuels. You succeeded in eliminating all of my men, but that is not of consequence. They would have died anyway, as you and I both will. What happened to your 10:45 arrival time?" Kenneth did not rise to the bait, but Zarawani continued anyway. "You Americans are so arrogant. Did you not think that we would find out about your attempt to sabotage our operation? We have been closely following your movements ever since Thursday, and have constantly been on your trail. We heard every word of your plan, and adjusted our operation accordingly." Zarawani spat contemptuously at the ground. "So, now you die, and do not merit witnessing the single most important event in all history. You will not witness this great victory of Allah, for you will be dead long before then."

Zarawani's fingers tightened around the trigger. The shot that rang through the air was closely followed by a scream. The scream was Zarawani's. The elevator door had opened, and behind it a woman stood, pistol in hand. The shot punctured Zarawani's gun hand and pierced through to the bone, flinging his AK-74 to the ground.

"Right on time, Stephanie," Kenneth growled as he kicked the gun towards the opposite edge of the building.

"Well, I couldn't let you die now, could I?" Stephanie responded. Zarawani moaned, clutching his bloodied hand. Stephanie rushed at him and gave him a powerful kick that flung him onto the hard tiled floor of the deck.

"The chopper should be here any minute, help me tie him up." Zarawani's limp form lay unconscious on the ground.

A helicopter had come into focus, and was advancing toward the building through the clear night sky. Zarawani had woken up and had seemingly resigned himself to his bonds. Kenneth watched as he tested the rope, and failed to find any weakness. Then Zarawani spoke.

"Your wife promised to leave the city," he said slowly.

"Do you think he deserves an explanation, Stephanie?" Kenneth asked.

"Of course not," Stephanie said, "but let's tell him for the fun of it."

"Okay, go ahead," Kenneth replied, "I'll listen patiently.'""

"Thanks, love." Stephanie took a deep breath before she began to tell Zarawani the story. "Two months ago, the agency notified us that an agent inside one of the more mature terrorist organizations, implying your own, was intending to destroy a massive selection of us 'infidels'..."

"Wait, you work for the agency?" Zarawani said slowly.

"Yes, it took you a while to catch on," Stephanie retorted. "Now please, don't interrupt me, or you won't hear the rest of it. So as I was saying, once we got wind of the fact that you had plotted this terrorist attack, we decided that we needed to deal with this threat silently and efficiently. Silently, because the country needs to feel secure if this economic rejuvenation is to occur, and efficiently because we can't afford the loss of any life, as to *us* life is the most important commodity. We could have eliminated you, but in time someone else would have come to fill your shoes. You of course, predicted that we would intercept you, so you needed to find out as much as you could about the threat we posed to your operation. We used your desire for information against you.

"So two weeks ago, we had ironed out all of the kinks in the plan. We supplied you with information that was partly accurate, but contained the flaws that would eventually bring you down. Our source leaked the information into the terrorist circles that my husband, Kenneth, was going to handle the operation alone. We allowed you to bug our apartment. We told you that I was going to be out of town, which immediately cleared me from involvement in the operation.

"We acted out scenes that ensured you would bring as little back-up as possible, by telling you that only one of our men would be involved. We also caught you by surprise by allowing him to arrive a half hour early. But the essence of the plan was that you would be overconfident, and this is why you failed. You placed a bug in Kenneth's tuxedo when it was taken to the dry cleaning, and were listening to him earlier tonight. So, as soon as he had convinced you that he would be alone at ten to eleven, he allowed the tuxedo jacket to be left in the dining room. You call us arrogant? Well we may be, but you are naïve in thinking that the agency would send a single operative to eliminate you. You have failed.

The helicopter landed on an empty part of the massive deck, just next to the swimming pool, and well clear of the fireworks. Zarawani struggled as they hauled him onto the helicopter, but to no avail. The helicopter took off, and flew into the dark night sky. An hour later thousands of people cheered as fireworks filled the skies over central park with hundreds of beautiful lights.

* * *

Stephanie Samuels sat at the dining room in The Sky Marriott. The place had made a killing, and was constantly improving its services, and talks of expansion were well underway. Kenneth sat opposite her, and watched as she cut into her rare filet mignon. Last time she had come here, she had been denied the right to have meat, for as in order to make her personality seem more timid, she had acted as a vegetarian. Now, she was here again with her husband, as well as her boss Khaled Ahmed, the chairman of the agency.

"So sorry to interrupt your sabbatical," he said, "but there are some more of those terrorists out there trying to make us Muslims look bad."

YELLOWHAMMER
Kiera M.

16 (F) of Co. Antrim, Northern Ireland

My golden, little Yellowhammer,
Singing gracefully from the hedge,
Don't let the sound of a hedge cutter
Fill your song with dread!
Sing to me your repertoire,
As you tilt your gilded head,
Or venture into the sunlight
And build your nest instead.

My golden, little Yellowhammer,
You never seem to rest!
Plucking at the grass,
Collecting twigs for your nest!
As I gaze in awe at you,
You draw a beady eye on me,
And with your little beak full,
You glide into the tree.

My golden, little Yellowhammer,

An intruder is coming near!
I tell you to run, he'll kill you,
But you're paralyzed in fear!
As the chainsaw revs and growls,
You bravely protect your nest.
If only, little Yellowhammer,
You knew it would be your death!

My golden, little Yellowhammer,
Where is your wonderful song?
Now the broken hedge is silent
And this stillness is so wrong!
In the place of your leafy home,
Now runs an evil winding path.
How could someone do this?
You suffered under his wrath.

My golden, little Yellowhammer,
How I wish I could hear you sing!
How I wish I could see you preen
Your feathered tawny wing!
And now my heart is silent,
Still without your song,
Hedgerows will never be the same,
Now that the Yellowhammer is gone.

LEARNING TO FLY
Sarah D.

20 (F) of New South Wales, Australia

Her hands had always been cold; they curled around my warm palm to thaw the ice. I used to think it was because she was outside a lot; her nose would go red and her breath was always laboured. I felt like all little girls were this way. Then she would come in and the snow would melt in her hair, little rivulets of ice water sliding down her face. It made her look wild and I loved her for it. That seemed to be the only thing I could love her for, one thing to grasp and breathe in. I could keep those moments inside me without thinking about who she was, how she invaded my life so completely.

Now I couldn't warm those hands, though I ran my own over them and clutched them to my lips, breathing my life against smooth palms. Her fingers were pale; a soft white that freckled up her arms – mother called them sun kisses, the freckles. Mother would look out into the white, watching the swirl of her only girl and laugh, talking about how she was sent from God to save us. She was sweet, lying there, though there was no movement beneath the thick quilt. There was no hint of saviour in the sallow cheeks of this girl; a dampened angel on the edge of nothing. She was almost lost in the quilt, and it swallowed her up to her chin, crowding around her skin in a swirl of dark blue. Mother used to say she looked like the moon when she was in her bed, a silent blush of white against the dense colour of the sky.

Purity, grace and skill were things my mother cherished. Her birth children were none of these things, gawky and long limbed we were crosses between walkers and fliers. Mother also said her daughter was destined for great things, because of how she looked. We were dark haired, thin lips with sharp noses; I'd stopped caring about the hawk in me. She'd look at us, my mother, and say that we looked like the dirt we were born from; cold and lifeless. She tried to explain what she meant in the only way she knew how, not knowing it made us hate her more. When I was seven she sat my brother and me down at the table and thumped a Bible against the lacquered surface.

"God, He doesn't love you."

God only pictured in her tales when she thought He wouldn't be listening – how she defined such times was beyond me.

"He took you from the earth and moulded you into hawk-people. Hawks, they're messengers, you hear?" She asked like we knew the answer, like she wanted an answer, but she ignored our open mouths and continued. "He doesn't love you like He does the real people, because you're messengers. You've got to know your place, and it isn't with Him, or with normal people. You'd be flying if He loved you, you'd be flying or you'd be back in the ground." My brother huddled himself against the chair, pushing himself as far as space would allow. He didn't dare move the chair from her; else the belt would appear in her hand fast, like it lived there. "I don't know why He chose me to birth dirt-hawks, but He did. I'm blessed because He chose me and cursed because He chose you."

She stood there; hand on the Bible's engraved cover, and stared at us over the steel of her glasses. She had brown eyes and I wondered then if that meant she was born a dirt-hawk too. The silence held, my brother not looking up and me gazing into those brown eyes and wondering. Her face flushed a dark red and she tore the Bible from its place and stalked from the room. The slamming door made us both relax and breathe.

I remember how my brother moved then, like he'd never walked a day in his life, stumbling from the table and retching in the kitchen sink. He never did love mother quite so well after that and I think she knew. I felt for her, stuck in the snow and the cold with two boys she never wanted, and never loved, with eyes that told her she was a dirt-hawk. She hated herself as much as she hated us, I think, and it forced her hand.

She loved Tahlia though, with a kind of pressure that filled the house with an awkward tension. Tahlia wasn't mother's; perhaps that was why she never hated her. When the thud of her body against the door woke me the first time, I was sixteen. There had been no storms but she felt like marble; cold and hard when I picked her up and took her inside. She was tiny as well, just a bundle of blonde hair in my arms.

We reckoned Tahlia was about six the first time, before she bolted. Soon as she got the legs to run, she was out the door and back into the woods, like some unsprung deer herding itself back home. Mother broke her best belt on Sean's back that night, like it was his fault she ran. By then, mother didn't touch me with the belt, I'd grown too tall, too strong, and she feared me somewhat. You could tell though her eyes, muddy as they were, and the panic when I hefted the axe, or the way she tensed when I moved behind her.

"You're a messenger, boy. Don't forget your place."

"Messengers need the strength to fly, don't they, mother? How else could God trust them?"

"Don't blaspheme in this house, boy! We don't use the Lord's name where it isn't needed." It was always needed when she wanted it to be. "And don't you talk back to your mother. I gave birth to you, ungrateful child." I assumed it was the parental lament wherever you went, a mother's guilt trip to anyone daring enough to talk back.

"Should we fall, mother, from His Grace, and His love, and His sight? Perhaps that would be best for His messengers to not be able to do His work?" She was livid, the hard curve of her mouth thinning as the corners of her eyes followed suit. "Perhaps you could explain to Him how you forbade me from my duties? How your hand slew my brother's back until he was a cripple, hardly worth the listening?" Her hand dipped into the draw at her side and pulled the Bible from its depths. "Will you mark me with His words?" She let her hand fall onto the table and stared at the simple flowers next to the thick book. Turning so her nose was against my cheek, she scowled. Her body was twisted oddly as her hand still clutched the Bible but her face and body turned into me. She seemed part serpent and part hawk; her eyes solid and focused on staring me down. She did that a lot - stare at me. Sometimes her eyes were blank and unfocused, but mostly they watched too closely to be anything but scrutiny.

"You will close your mouth, child, and go back to the habits that you have. I will not be spoken to this way." Her voice, cold and somehow detached, felt like a slice of pain in my ears.

I walked away.

Months later, Tahlia crouched in the corner of our porch. I found her there at the same time as she woke, her eyes blinking and rolling in their sockets, her blue lips breaking apart with a thin scratch and tear. The blood threw me, how it beaded between the craggy rises of skin, so I kept my eyes away from her face as I lifted her. Inside the house my mother was already preparing Tahlia's bed, having seen me pushing the door open. I wondered at that point where my brother was, but I didn't suppose it mattered so much as to let myself be distracted.

I feel such a deep regret for that. I believe that regret, mingled with an intimate guilt, will continue for a very long time. Mother told us we were messengers, His messengers. I have always wondered if that was something she merely wished was true, or if it was His doing. When Tahlia was asleep I left my mother in the chair by her side and looked for my brother. Sean was younger than me by two years; his short black hair habitually covered his murky brown eyes until my mother screeched for him to cut it.

That night his hair was choppy and uneven, slurring out from his face in bloody clots. It amazed me that his pulse was thick, though his eyes blinked at me before shuddering away. It was easy to lift him back onto his bed, he'd grown so thin, ignoring the spreading pink-red. I rolled him on his face to see his shirt was gone, through the stickiness I felt coarse fabric patterned into the swollen welts; pulling the fibres further into his skin. I dashed out to collect a bowl and water, returning to notice the dampness of the pillow. Ignoring the tears, I tried not to throw up; the blood put out a sickly sweet odour that seemed to climb into my body and my senses. My nostrils flared and my eyes rolled, I'd have dropped the bowl had Sean not whimpered as my breath hit his exposed back. It was an empty, lost noise that forced my eyes open and my hands steady.

Washing Sean's back was hard. Each press of the cloth made his muscles spasm and with each tense gathering of muscle, blood welled and pooled in each cut. I could see the hairs on his knuckles as they rose in pain and the way his nails bit into the wooden bedpost. When the water was a thick pink, I began to peel the fabric from his skin. We both knew that any noise - anything louder than usual -would bring mother to his bedside, so we flirted with silence. I worried that the openings would become infected; some pieces I couldn't detach from his skin, and each wound bled as I worked.

There was a long strip of burlap beaten next to his spine, the piece was thin but covered the middle ten centimetres of skin. My fingers scrabbled in Sean's blood, feeling the exposed knots of muscle and veins, but the end of the fabric was mashed into his body. There were grains of wheat sewn into the slices; they seemed as though they belonged. I found an edge of the fabric and flinched as a weak cry hesitated from Sean's lips; his whole body seizing as I lifted it. My flinch pulled on the fabric, and the sickly wet sound of tearing met us both. His back moved suddenly, a lift and twist that ripped the fabric from the skin and ended with a shudder of blood and muscle. His tears stopped then, and I watched his eyes roll back to their whites, feeling his body slump against the mattress. My fingernails were rimmed in red, and I collected my things to swap for clean tools. When I returned with a clean bowl, ready to re-wash his back, my mother was there.

"Get up! Filthy dirt-hawk, you're ruining my sheets! How ungrateful you are! Pathetic child; weeping tears on my pillows, bleeding on my sheets, you should have stayed where I left you." Sean wasn't conscious to hear it, which felt a lot better than it should have. I shuffled, re-arranging the bowl in my hands, as she turned to glare at me. "Get out."

"I doubt either of us thinks I'm going to go." I walked to the bed and she leaned her body away from mine.

"How dare you disobey your own mother? I work hard to keep you both clothed and fed, and this is how I am repaid? The Lord let you come to life, and this is how you thank his vessel? You both disgust me."

"Not quite so disgusting as beating your own child. Did you use the burlap to try and hide it?" Mother's knees shuddered, making her dip before she locked them tight. "Do you think the Lord approves, mother? Do you think he is smiling down upon his vessel with love and adoration? His messenger is crippled. He may not walk again; did you not watch how close you came to his spine?" Her mouth shifted and her tongue rolled against her cheek. "Perhaps we should leave him to die, and let God know his vessel failed."

"Fix your brother, dirt-hawk, and do not speak to me again." She walked with a jerky hip movement that said she was unsure, holding in her wish to run.

Tahlia stayed longer this time, moving around the house and exploring with wide, excited eyes. She never spoke, though, and my mother spoke of the hawk-curse damaging her new child. Tahlia could never have been a hawk, mother beamed, she was so much more. It didn't last. While Sean recuperated in his room, walking only short distances in the weeks after the last beating he would ever experience, Tahlia ran away.

Mother wasn't livid. Her hands clutched the Bible to her chest as she went about her business, but she never spoke a word of blame. I knew then that my mother loved Tahlia – which is the name we gave her after a time, though no-one could remember why – more than she ever had her real sons. We all expected Tahlia to return soon, to find her crouched on our porch in the snow. It was almost a year, though, until we saw her again.

She walked to our door in the still summer air and knocked, a sharp rap of her knuckles against wood. I motioned her in as my mother cried out in delight, sweeping Tahlia up into her arms and hugging her. By then, Sean was walking well, though he was perpetually curved so that he hunched in on himself. Tahlia spoke perfectly, her eyes flicking from one of us to the other. "I would like to live here."

The request was abrupt but mother accepted immediately. She watched Tahlia's happy cheeks grow with a smile, before running to prepare her room. Sean accepted Tahlia just as easily, letting her small hands stroke his back as she hugged him. Maybe it was that I was unused to such an amiable female, but I distrusted her little girl eyes, and the innocence in her smile. I was right to keep my trust from her... but not right to deny her the opportunity to win it. She didn't hug me that day, nor any day after that. I held her hand when she needed me to, and watched over her as she lived, and loved, in our little house. Sean taught her how to read quietly to herself from the Bible, teaching her his favourite passages, and mother seemed happier every day that Tahlia stayed. It was four years before we went back to how it was, three of us keeping house far away from any kind of life. I told my mother that everything would go wrong some day, that Tahlia couldn't be perfect, and our home could not stay a home so long. Maybe that is what she meant when she called us messengers, we speak the truth when we are able. I spoke it.

Tahlia caught a cold, the snow melting down her nape and into her lungs, it seemed. Mother was annoyed but accepting, looking after the angel she never had. Sean worked hard to cheer the young girl, always putting on voices and playing so that she felt like normal. After two weeks, mother began to worry, her girl was getting worse and there was little that was working. When I looked in on Tahlia, my heart jumped. She was thin and pale even when well, but surrounded by the colour and clutter of her room, she seemed to shrink. There were purple flowers dying on her window sill and the train that Sean carved. My heart wanted to burst out and walk across that room to smash the vase the flowers were in. The train was delicate and beautiful, like the room itself, with the arches and tidy nooks, and it made me angrier than I had ever been.

This little girl had stolen a childhood from me that I never expected I could have owned. Turning around, I ignored the hate and anger, and strode down the hall to meet my mother at the stairs. The polished banister was glossy under the hallway window and I wanted to stop and explore the patterns of the light. Mother stopped with me and looked toward Tahlia's room.

"She's not getting better. I'm worried she won't make it." There was a softness in her voice that I rarely heard, that I'd never heard in my childhood. It made me tired, my body heavy and exhausted with the pressure of the emptiness inside me. I wasn't sure how the emptiness came to be, exactly, or how it weighted me so that when I swayed at the stair I didn't fall.

Mother did, though. She fell and tumbled down the stairs until the wet thud of her body at the bottom filled me with something more than hate. Relief. Relief centred me as my body travelled down to look at her pale face. Her neck was broken, her head lying at odd angles to the rest of her. I considered how I didn't hear it break while I watched the blood seep from her eye; her glasses smashed into her nose. Sean stood next to me and watched her as well. It was like we were waiting for mother to stand up again, Bible in hand, and tell us we were dirt hawks.

She didn't get up.

BRANDING
Kristin O.

19 (F) of Colorado, USA

I made an indentation on the world;

I carved my initials into its soul

And left my mark.

I was the song that played in its dreams

For one night.

I was the ink-stain on its weathered pages –

A stately sentence, a stamp of purpose on the paper.

I stood and screamed into the sky

And the world heard me.

I slid across the world's heartstrings

And made a melody that lingered

Like snowflakes in the sky.

I burned myself into its crust –

The messy and the mundane and the magnificent –

All of it, scorched onto the skin of the earth.

I was the scab on the surface of the world;

Itchy and crusted black with burnt-out dreams,

And the weariness of words not heard.

I was the scar that formed when the scab was scratched;

Pink flesh faintly puckered with remembered pain,

Stretched and smoothed by the slow passage of time.

I was the smear of dirt,

The stain of quirks and confusion,

Of irrational anger and hysteria.

I was music and midnight,

Hope and despair,

Fear and strength.

I scarred and sang and screamed;

I broke and blackened and scorched;

I laughed and loved and lived,

And the world saw.

The world remembered.

I was here.

LADY UNICORN
Karina O.

21 (F) of California, USA

Eleanor liked the way her husband smelled. It was a strange mixture of sweat, soap, and axle grease, from working on cars all day long. Now he was asleep, his damp hair ruffled by the pillowcase. He had been tossing and turning, and from the soft moonlight that stole through the blinds, she could see that his face had turned rigid. He was clenching his teeth.

She brushed her hand over his ears, letting her fingers comb through his thin hair. He moved slightly at her touch, and for a moment she thought he would wake up.

"Love?" she murmured. Her voice sounded half-asleep.

Still, he smiled and turned towards her. A gentle snore came from him, vibrating the walls of the room, followed by another of even greater proportions. She listened to him for a minute, letting her breathing fall in sync with his snoring.

"Love?" she murmured again. Her lips trembled. "I can't sleep."

Her voice was soft, too soft to wake him up, but that was okay. She didn't want to disturb him. He had gone to bed early, sleeping from a hard day's work, and soon he would wake up again, only to work another day and come back home, coated with new stains and smells from his job. Every night, he washed himself, scrubbing his oily, dark skin into a soft pink, but though the stains always disappeared, the smell never seemed to wash away.

His face was passive and so at ease that she couldn't resist smiling, reaching out to stroke his cheek. Her fingers bumped along the bristles of his unshaven face. "I think I had a bad day," she admitted in a whisper, leaning closer to him so her face nearly touched his. "I took Julia to the doctor today.

She has an ear infection. But the insurance won't pay for the medicine the doctor prescribed. They say it's nothing. They say that she'll get better. But I know she won't."

He gave a louder snore than usual.

She shivered and sat up quickly, afraid of waking him up, but after a moment, his body relaxed. Once more, she hovered just above his face, brushing back her long hair. "She's deaf. She can barely hear what I say. You remember how she loved music, more than anything? She can't hear it. It's nothing to her."

Her voice felt raw, and besides, she was getting too shrill anyway. She stopped talking and rubbed her throat instead. Once more she forced herself to breathe with his snoring.

For a minute, all she concentrated on was him and soon she felt her eyes close. Colors played across her eyelids, green and yellow dots dancing the blackness. Once more, she snuggled beside him, burying her head into his chest. She sighed.

She might have fallen asleep, but a second later, a sharp whistle coming out from her husband's nose. She jerked up and gave a cry, clutching the blankets around her tightly. Then, after realizing what the whistle was and how loud she must have cried, she clamped a hand over her mouth, her face turning red.

But her husband didn't hear her and the snoring continued anew. Except now she couldn't sleep.

Eleanor listened to him for several more minutes and tried to keep quiet. She rocked back and forth, shivering, her hands rubbing her sleek polyester sleeves of her nightgown. There she stayed until a sick lurch came to her stomach. She leaned closer to her husband. "I think it's much worse than just an ear infection," she confessed. She reached out to touch her husband's shoulders, but he turned away from her, rolling onto his other side.

He stopped snoring.

Though she knew that he was only asleep and he would not be able to hear her anyway, a terrible pang of loneliness hit her. She crawled off the bed and stood up, her pink nightgown a pale gray. She shivered and cast a glance at her husband. He was huddled in his blankets, only the tiniest bit of his face showing. In the moonlight, he looked like a ghost.

For a moment, she just stood there, watching him. Then, carefully so she would not wake him, she crept out of the room and into the hallway.

In the daylight, the hallway beamed of colors, from the family photos that hung neatly on the walls to the blue shag carpets covering the oak floor.

But at night, the moon cast an eerie glow on everything so that the colors were weird and distorted. She blinked, adjusting her eyes to the pale light, and tiptoed through the hallway, her fingers trailing over the frames and faces of her family.

Usually when she looked at the photographs, the first thing she noticed was her husband's beaming face, which she found handsome, even after seven years of marriage. But now, Julia's face poked out. There was Julia as she first walked. Julia, being kissed by her father, who had a dark oil stain on his nose. Julia, playing with a stuffed doggy. Julia…

But the photograph that attracted Eleanor the most was the one with her by the ocean. Julia was holding up a conch shell to her ear and had the most surprised, most delighted look on her face. "Look Mommy!" Julia had cried, just before the picture had been taken, small waves rushing to her ankles as she stood barefoot in the wet sand. "I can hear the ocean!" It was the most perfectly ridiculous thing that Eleanor had ever heard, and she quickly beckoned her husband to snap a picture. And now the moment was forever frozen in time.

She fingered the frame and sighed, glancing around. The curtains were drawn, as they always were at night, and she could see a bit of orange poking out from the streetlight. She considered going to Julia's room, to check up on her, but just the thought of that made Eleanor shiver.

No.

She would let Julia sleep in peace. Besides, she wouldn't be able to help her anyway. Julia was drugged up on cough syrup and pills already. No, Eleanor's place was back in her husband's room. There, the blankets were warm and his thick musty smell engulfed the room. That was where she belonged. She shivered again and began to tiptoe back to the room, but something made her hesitate.

She heard something.

At first, she thought she was just imagining the noise. It wasn't very loud, only a faint throbbing in her ears, and if it weren't so cold and strange in the deserted hallway, she guessed she might have missed it entirely. Still, as the pulse echoed across the hallway, interrupting the gentle snores of her husband, a surge of panic rushed through her.

It was music, only music. In a way, it reminded her of the times she had gotten songs playing endlessly in her head, except that this song came from outside. And though this music was strange, more of a rhythm than an actual melody, there was something familiar about it.

The music swelled, its pulse ringing through her entire body. As it came closer, the moonlight seemed to intensify and the small orange streetlight waned through the curtain.

Her knees trembled, but she forced herself to stand up straight. Slowly, she crept to the curtain, her hands shaking as they grasped the seams of the rough fabric. For a minute, she forced herself to breathe deeply in, her breath automatically in sync with the pulsing beat she heard from outside. Finally, when she could bear it no longer, she jerked open the curtains. And then she gasped.

She saw a unicorn.

At first, Eleanor just stared. She wanted to believe that it was just a white deer, or maybe a horse, but something about this beast was so different from either, so lovely that the mere sight of it sent a surge of both panic and wild joy into her throat that...

She pressed her face close to the window and watched.

The unicorn was outside just below the streetlight, jumping up and down on her hind legs fending off invisible foes, twisting her head around so that her alicorn spun in the air, creating small white sparks. As Eleanor squinted, she realized that the unicorn was fighting (playing?) with the moths gathered near the dull orange streetlight. As the unicorn jumped up and sailed near the moths, the moths fluttered toward her, and then it was a race! The unicorn leapt, ecstatic as her neat cloven hooves kicked out into the air among the moths. The more she jumped, the more the pulsing in Eleanor's body throbbed until it became apparent that the pulsing was not her head or even her body, but her heart.

Eleanor wanted to meet her. She strained at the window, her breath fogging up the glass, until at last the music became too much, and she raced to the nearest door, stumbling out onto her front lawn. It was dark – everywhere the unicorn didn't touch was dark – but that didn't stop her and she continued blindly on until at last, the light shone on brightly before her and she was close, very close, to the unicorn.

It was then that she regained her senses, and realized just how long and sharp the unicorn's alicorn was and how strong and graceful the unicorn had kicked out as she had played (fought?) with the moths. And as these thoughts came across her mind, Eleanor realized how blind and ugly she was in the unicorn's presence and how her much knees trembled.

The unicorn had stopped moving and she lightly stepped forward towards Eleanor, the blades of grass barely moving under her weight. Eleanor brushed off her flimsy pink nightgown, thick with the strange smell of sweat, soap, and axle grease.

"Have you come for me?"

The unicorn stopped and tilted her head. It was apparent from her soulful blue eyes that yes, she did understand Eleanor, but she didn't say anything. Instead, Eleanor felt an uncomfortable tickle of joy rush through her body.

She tried again. "Have you come for me?" Somewhere in the back of her mind, a spot of information about unicorn lore sprang up. "I'm not a virgin, you know." Her voice wavered as she said this and suddenly she felt ashamed, but the unicorn only seemed to smile at her words.

It was quiet for a moment and Eleanor nervously patted down her hair, so it wasn't so wild. She paused, waiting for the unicorn to speak. Her knees trembled.

"Perhaps you want to see my daughter?" she finally asked, her voice soft and breathless. "She is sick. If you want to, you can help her. Come! I'll show you where she is."

But the unicorn didn't move and her lovely blue eyes remained impassive. A fresh wave of desperation hit Eleanor. "You don't understand," Eleanor whispered to the unicorn. "She can't hear music."

The unicorn snorted at this and then, as a response, stamped her tiny cloven hoof into the ground. An avalanche of music hit Eleanor, so strange and wild that she couldn't help but hide her head, her fingers plugging up her ears. But the music was much too loud to ignore. She cried out desperately for it to stop, but her cry only added to the chord echoing out all around her. And then, suddenly, it was quiet.

She could still hear the music throbbing in her head, and it was a minute before she dared to unplug her ears. She was still trembling – it was impossible not to – but she didn't know whether it was from excitement or anxiety. She cast an uncertain look at the unicorn, a blush suddenly spreading across her face, but the unicorn didn't move, her tail only swatting the moths away.

"So this is music?" Eleanor rubbed her face and shivered. "I never heard anything like that before. I'm not quite sure I like it. But it was loud. Do you think Julia heard it?"

The unicorn tossed her mane into the air and neighed harshly. Eleanor backed away.

"Oh, what a silly question," she muttered, twisting her hands together. "Of course she heard it. The music, that is. Didn't she? It would be impossible not to hear it."

And suddenly, Eleanor knew that Julia was all right and when she woke up tomorrow, everything would be fine. Tears filled her eyes. "You've healed her, haven't you?" she said, her voice choking. "That's why you're here. You came to help my daughter. You didn't have to, but you did anyway. And I suppose you'll be leaving now, won't you?"

A gentle look came into the unicorn's eyes. She pawed the ground again and lowered her head submissively to Eleanor.

Come to me.

Eleanor hesitated at first, unwilling to come to the unicorn in case she would just bolt away, but the more she resisted the unicorn, the more her heartbeat pulsed until she thought she would die if she could never meet the unicorn. Her knees buckled and she stumbled blindly to the unicorn, her bare feet crunching into the grass.

It seemed to take forever, but finally Eleanor felt her soft fur tickling her fingertips. She laughed and wrapped her arms around the unicorn's neck, burying her hands into the mane. The mane flowed like white liquid over her fingers.

"You're beautiful," she whispered.

The unicorn sighed, flicking her tail. Her eyes fluttered close and, carefully so she would not hurt Eleanor with her long, spiraling alicorn, she rubbed her cheek on Eleanor's.

Eleanor frowned.

She stepped away from the unicorn, looking down at her critically. Finally, ever so slowly, she let her hand go to the unicorn's forehead and traced the spiral upwards until she got to the very tip of the alicorn.

"This isn't real, is it? It's just a dream. I'll wake up and you'll be gone and they'll be nothing left."

The unicorn said nothing but bowed her head more, the tip of her alicorn hovering above Eleanor's hand. Eleanor frowned and watched as the unicorn slid her alicorn through her hand. And then she gasped.

Blood rushed out of her index finger, first only a couple of drops, but after a couple of seconds, it flowed like water. She stuck it her mouth to stop the bleeding, but that didn't help any. The more she sucked on her finger, the more she felt the salty stickiness of her blood coat her mouth until at last she gasped and choked. Her knees buckled and she collapsed onto the crunchy grass.

And it hurt.

She glanced at her hand, which now lay in a puddle of blood on the lawn, and shivered. "You've killed me," she murmured.

The unicorn frowned at this and lifted up her alicorn high, so that it would not touch Eleanor, and gently bent down to rub her furry cheek onto Eleanor's finger. At first, this hurt even more, and it was all Eleanor could do but to hold onto the unicorn's mane, but eventually, the pain subsided and the most delicious sensation bubbled up in her. She smiled and took her finger off the unicorn's cheek, inspecting it once more. It had healed completely, and even the scar from a wart she had since she was seven had disappeared. She flexed her hand experimentally and smiled, looking at the unicorn once more. A red star stained the unicorn's cheek.

"What now?" The unicorn neighed weakly and shook her mane. She looked dazed at first, and Eleanor noticed how the lovely unicorn's slender knees wobbled. She went to help her, but the unicorn just shook her away. In another minute, the unicorn reared up, giving out a neigh that sounded more like a roar, and raced away.

Eleanor couldn't help herself – she stumbled after the unicorn, following the flickering white tail that lingered just ahead of her. The rhythm pulsed all around her, keeping in time with her heartbeat, and off in the distance, she was sure she heard a melody, though she wasn't sure if it wasn't the whistling in her ears as the wind rushed past or something else. But that didn't matter. Music or not, her bare feet thudded along the asphalt to the song, her laughter and gasps accompaniment.

There were only several times during the race where a feeling of hopelessness came, and that was only when the unicorn disappeared behind a tree, and Eleanor couldn't see her. But a moment later, the unicorn poked out from the brush and the chase continued in earnest. In this manner, they raced across town, from the suburban playground to the downtown pet store, and even across the office park.

It was just outside of a fast-food restaurant where Eleanor finally caught up with the unicorn. She crashed into her, barreling her head into the unicorn's soft belly, and both of them fell, a tangle of fur and polyester. Eleanor giggled, though she hardly knew why, and rubbed her face on the unicorn's belly, enjoying and the salty taste lingering on the unicorn's fur and the satiny feel of each of the individual strands as they tickled her nose. The unicorn licked her ear gently and Eleanor smiled, a wild look coming into her eyes.

"I caught you," Eleanor said, her voice breathless. "I caught you and now you have to do whatever I say." The unicorn didn't say anything to this. "Stand up."

At first, Eleanor was afraid that the unicorn would not follow her directions and pierce her with that lovely alicorn, but the unicorn obediently stood up, looking down at Eleanor with a gentle patience. Eleanor scrambled up and mounted onto the unicorn, as if the unicorn were just a simple horse, letting her fingers twist around the unicorn's lovely mane. "Let's ride."

The unicorn hesitated at her words, but a moment later, Eleanor felt the unicorn's muscles tightened. The unicorn leapt forward, but it was much faster and farther than Eleanor had expected and if it weren't for her fingers, twined deeply into the unicorn's mane, she was sure she would have fallen off. Her stomach dropped and she pressed her cheek onto the unicorn's neck, staring down. The world blurred beneath her.

It was only a couple of seconds, though it felt like an eternity, and when they landed, Eleanor felt a wave of relief wash over her. She was about to roll off, to tell the unicorn that she had enough, but before she could say anything, the unicorn leapt into the air again. And again. The next leap was just as bad, but by the third time, her free hand reached for the moon and stars.

After the sixth leap, the unicorn stopped and Eleanor was exhausted. She was still happy, and the music pulsed stronger in her ears, but her mind spun with so many colors that she felt dizzy. She closed her eyes and sighed. Her white hands loosened and she slumped over, sliding off the unicorn's smooth back.

She fell on something soft.

She wanted to sleep, but the unicorn nudged her awake, tickling her with her velvet muzzle. It was dark, and Eleanor first tried to turn away from the unicorn, but the unicorn only stepped over her, her alicorn gently tapping Eleanor's eyelids.

Wake up.

But it wasn't the unicorn that woke her up. No. The music was stronger here, and the steady rhythm throbbed in her ears and surrounded her. It didn't sound like a heartbeat anymore. Instead it was a gentle breathing, and as every pulse came, a wave of salty moisture accompanied it, penetrating itself in every pore of her skin.

She yawned, stretching. As she lifted herself up, she noticed the ground slip by her fingers, shifting with every movement she put on it. Sand. She yawned again and brushed off her mouth, tiny grains falling from her lips. The air was thick and salty. It tasted like fish. Eleanor smiled and looked up at the unicorn, standing just above her.

"The ocean."

The unicorn nodded and looked away from Eleanor, out to something else. Eleanor turned her head to follow the direction of the alicorn and smiled.

The ocean was black still, but moonlight reflected on it, revealing tiny white caps as the waves broke on the shore. Eleanor glanced over the waves briefly and turned to the sky and its million dancing stars. She smiled. "It's pretty."

The unicorn said nothing to this. Instead, she nuzzled her blood-stained cheek into Eleanor's shoulder and stepped out cautiously into the water. There, she turned back to Eleanor and gave a soft but urgent whinny. Eleanor frowned.

"What's the matter?"

The unicorn looked to the ocean at first and then back to Eleanor, her face desperate. She lifted up her cloven hoof and pawed at the water. But something was wrong with her. Her delicate cloven hoof was melting into the water. She still could stand, as long as she was in the water, but no more could she walk on land. White capped waves tossed onto the shore, their little peaks like smooth horse heads, coming to the land. And suddenly Eleanor understood.

She stepped back.

"No," she murmured slowly.

The unicorn was still staring at her, her lovely blue eyes piercing through Eleanor. With every tremble of her ribs came another rush of waves (unicorns?) at her delicate cloven hooves. The music was stronger now, and for the first time, Eleanor could hear the entire song in its entirety. The unicorns were singing the rhythm, and the stars were dancing to it, and the melody? The melody…

She was the melody.

"No," she whispered, her lovely treble voice wavering in a vibrato. "No, you must understand. My daughter. My lovely daughter, Julia. She needs my help. And my husband! I can't leave him."

The unicorns (waves?) crashed on the shores again, this time circling around her ankles. But before going back, the waves tugged at the unicorn, her unicorn, and tried to drag her back into the sea as well. The unicorn, her unicorn, cried a sharp whinny and stumbled, desperately trying to stand. Eleanor trembled and almost stepped forward to the sea, to the music, to…

The unicorns retreated and, for now, her unicorn was safe. But it was only temporarily, Eleanor knew. The tide was drifting away, and soon her unicorn would go away with it.

And she would never see her lovely unicorn again.

Eleanor closed her eyes tightly, trying to stifle her tears. "No, I can't go, you must understand." Her voice sounded strange and cracked. She stepped forward to the unicorn and put her arms around the unicorn's neck, rubbing her face with the unicorn's blood-stained cheek. "You must understand! I can't leave. Not now. Not when I'm needed."

Come follow me.

"No."

It was barely a whisper, but Eleanor could see the unicorn shiver as she said this. She peered at Eleanor's blotched face carefully before finally nodding, tears filling up her eyes. A strange choked whinny came from her, but she seemed to smile anyway, letting her alicorn stroke Eleanor's cheek.

Eleanor shuddered and backed away.

She didn't get far. She stared at the unicorn, her unicorn, twisting her hands together. The unicorn sighed and then bowed low, her body melting into the tide, and for a second, the two met again, the unicorn washing over Eleanor's feet.

And then she was gone.

Wet sand clung to Eleanor's ankles, even as she stumbled onto the dry loose sand. She was crying bitterly, tears pouring from her eyes, and it was all she could do but throw herself on the cold dry sand and bury her head in her arms. She cried for a long time – it felt like hours – but eventually, her body relaxed, with the lullaby from the unicorns rushing on the shore, her head pulsing with rhythm and her mind dancing with stars…

Then, slowly, the sand melted away and in its place, she felt her cold fingers clutching soft shag carpets instead. And though her lips still tasted salty, a familiar smell wafted to her, one of sweat, soap, and axle grease. In the back of her mind, she could still hear the pulsing rhythm pounding through her head, but the more she concentrated on it, the more it slipped away, like water through sand. The music was replaced by her husband's monotonous snoring.

She smiled and fell asleep.

ORANGE PEEL AND APPLE PIPS
Heather W.

19 (F) of North Yorkshire, England

There must be more to life than this:
a winter wind and withered kiss
upon these frozen, sun-parched lips;
just orange peel and apple pips.

We're living on remains of death
with bottle caps, recycled breath,
and feeble rays of advent light
illuminate brash Beauty's blight.

There's less to love than fragile Rose
who blooms in seldom summer prose.
We're nothing more than drops and blips;
just orange peel and apple pips.

AZALEAS FOR SUSIE
Kelley D.

20 (F) of New York, USA

It rained the morning you were born.

I was six, and furious with our parents for daring to have another child. They had our older brother—the golden-haired, athletic son any parents would boast of—and they had me—the brunette musician with a flair for the dramatic.

Luke's hair wound itself into tight ringlets in the evening after his bath, softening to gentler waves by morning. My hair was straight, and I always insisted on wearing it parted on the side, with a matching barrette to hold it out of my face. We were lovely children—why did they need you?

Eight-year old Luke wore his racecar pajamas that morning. He lay on his stomach beside the Christmas tree and indolently flicked at the ornaments on the lowest branches.

"Mommy hates it when you do that," I informed him from my seat at the piano. My feet dangled in the air.

"Mind your own business," he said. He flicked another ornament, then sighed and rolled over onto his back. He yelled the babysitter's name, and asked if he could go outside and play.

"No, you can't," I said. "Because—"

"I know, I know," he cut me off. "Because it's raining. I can see out the window just as good as you."

"But it's not just raining. It's pouring. It's raining cats and dogs. It's a monsoon, it's a flood, it's a disaster!" I hopped off the piano bench and padded across the floor to sit beside him. "It will rain for days—days and days and days—and we will wonder if there was ever a time when it wasn't raining."

Luke had been scowling at first, but when he realized that I had begun one of my stories, he smiled a little, and rolled onto his stomach, looking up at me.

Delighted at holding my big brother's attention, I continued. "We'll have to leave this house, and find higher ground. It will be someplace far, far away from here, and we will probably never be able to return. It will be a great tragedy for our city—probably the whole state. And if the rain doesn't let up, the whole world! Not very many people will survive."

Luke rolled over onto his back again, tapping an ornament with one finger, watching it swing back and forth. Outside, it rained harder.

"But our whole family will make it to a safe place, and we'll build a new house. Probably not as big as this one, or as nice, but it will be safe, and it will be ours, and that will be enough."

Rain striking the window made an angry, percussive noise, and my words trailed off into nothingness. Moments later, the phone rang.

The peaceful moment shattered as Luke bolted from his place on the floor and dashed to the phone. "I GOT IT, I GOT IT!" he screamed, and picked up before the babysitter could.

He listened intently, then his face fell. "Oh. Cool." He handed the receiver to the babysitter and shuffled away. "It's a girl," he said.

"I guess they'll name her Susanna, like they wanted to."

"Guess so."

I sighed. "Even her name is better than mine."

"Do you think they'll call her Susie for short?" Luke asked, without much interest.

The gloomy expression on my face matched his. "Our lives are over," I said solemnly.

"I wanted it to be a boy," he said petulantly.

"Why are *you* so mad? At least you're still the only son. Now I'm the horrible older sister. They'll lock me away in a tower, with nothing to eat but crumbs! They'll raise *her* like she's a princess, and she'll wake every morning to beautiful music and I'll waste away to *nothing*." I moaned and hid my face in my hands.

"Oh, they'll give you more than crumbs," Luke said.

"That is not the point."

"Well…"

I looked up at him and flung my hands out in desperation. "Well what?"

"I'll bring you a grilled cheese."

I stared at him. "You can't."

"How come?"

"My tower will be far away from here, and very dangerous to travel to."

Luke shrugged. "So what? I can take a plane or something."

"But it will be heavily guarded, with poison thorns all around the bottom, and a mile high. You won't even be able to see the top of it from the ground."

"I can climb it," Luke said confidently.

I fingered one of the little bows on my nightgown. "You'd do that?" I asked him.

"Yeah. It'll be easy."

I sniffled. "I don't want to go to the tower."

"Hey." He put his arm around my shoulders. "Don't worry about it. If you have to go to the tower I'll come see you every day, and I'll always bring a grilled cheese."

"Promise?"

"I promise."

They brought you home the next day, around lunchtime. The roads were icy those few days before Christmas, so we didn't go see you in the hospital. I was angry with you, because I had decided that it was your fault I hadn't seen my mother for days. I don't remember much about our first meeting, except that I thought you thoroughly ordinary, and I pitied you for being born third, when Mommy and Daddy already had two wonderful children to compare you to.

At first, Luke and I did all we could to ignore you. But Luke was always intrigued by novelty, and within the first few hours of your arrival, he had already turned into another one of your minions, bowing and scraping and serving your every whim. By the end of the day, he loved you, and I was sick with envy at no longer holding the exclusive rights to his affection.

You cried every night the first week you were home. Luke never woke up, but I heard it—those irritating, piteous cries that lasted for hours—and I hated you even more.

I tried to pretend you didn't exist, but that soon proved impossible. By being born, you had earned a place in the hearts of every member of my family.

I didn't understand. All you did was coo and cry and scream and poop and spit and sleep and kick your fat legs. Anyone could do that.

I resented you for the next two years. Without ever trying, you were everybody's favorite. I didn't even care that my name was your first word.

"Marta," you said, and smiled up at me.

"My name," I informed you coolly, "is Martha."

"Marta," you repeated, waving your fat, baby fists.

Everyone was so excited about your first word that they all started calling me Marta. The name doesn't bother me anymore, but at the time, it was infuriating. It wasn't my real name, and all the adults in my life were making fools of me by indulging a baby who didn't know or care that she'd gotten her way.

My real reason for hating you, though, sprang from the fact that our family and friends had every reason to adore you: you were perfect.

It was as if our parents had taken all the good things about me, and all the good things about Luke, and watered down our bad qualities, and put them in this third child. The result was a harmonious mixing of hot and cold, light and dark.

Your hair, in contrast to Luke's blonde ringlets and my flat, dark hair, was a light, lovely shade of brown that framed your round little face in wispy waves. We all had dark brown eyes, but yours were loveliest of all—framed by thick, captivating, dark lashes. You were never as dramatic as me, but you were always animated, and people were drawn to you. You had Luke's natural athleticism, but at only two years old already wanted to learn to read and write. You were curious, charming, adorable, delightful.

In short, completely nauseating.

By the time you were three, you were speaking in full, cogent sentences, and you followed me everywhere.

I passed you sitting at the kitchen table, drawing fat clouds with a purple crayon.

"Where are you going?" you asked, swinging your feet back and forth.

"Outside."

"What are you gonna do?"

"Garden."

"Me too!" you squealed, dropping the crayon and wiggling out of your seat, following me out the back door and into the breezy spring afternoon. "What are we gonna garden?"

"*I* am going to pull weeds away from the flower bushes."

"What for?"

"To keep them away."

"Why?"

"Because they're bad."

"But why?"

"They just are, okay?"

"Okay."

I knelt down in front of one of the shrubs that lined the fence of our backyard and got to work. Dressed in a short-sleeved yellow dress with a tiny white bow on the collar, you squatted beside me and watched. For several minutes, you didn't say anything, and were very, very still.

Digging my fingers into the soil and grass, I turned my shoulder, and accidentally knocked a flower off the bush.

"What's that?" you asked, looking at the separated blossom with interest.

"Flower," I answered.

"What kinda flower?"

"A pink one."

"Rose. Daisy. Pink Flower."

I sighed and jerked the weed out of the ground, tossing it to the side. "No, that's not its *name*," I said.

"Oh. What's its name?"

"It's an azalea."

You frowned, and your lips slid into a half-pout of confusion.

I sighed. "Say it after me. Uh."

"Uh."

"Zayl."

"Zayl."

"Yuh."

"Yuh."

"Azaela."

"'Zaela."

I looked down at your little face, brows furrowed in concentration. You lifted hopeful eyes up to me. "Was that right, Marta?"

I shrugged. "Close enough."

You watched me pull up a few more weeds.

"Marta?"

"What."

"Can I have that 'zaela?"

"Sure."

Your face lit in a smile, and, lifting it with careful little fingers, placed it in the small pocket on the front of your dress. "Can I help?" you asked.

I shrugged again. "Okay."

When we went inside at dusk, we both had dirt on our faces and in our hair, and there was a hole in your dress where you'd snagged it on the fence. Our hands were filthy, our knees deeply matted with dirt.

Our mother didn't even scold us, just put us in the bathtub together and dumped in more bubble bath than we really needed.

"That was fun," you said, running your grimy hands back and forth under the water streaming from the faucet, watching the dirt run off your palms and into the bubbles.

It had been, but I didn't want to say so.

"Can I help again tomorrow?" you asked.

"I'm not going to do it again tomorrow," I said.

"Okay. But next time?"

Help might not be so bad, I thought. I had to pull the weeds anyway, because Daddy had made it my job. It had gone faster with you helping today anyway. You hadn't even annoyed me at all.

"If you want to. You know, Susie, I kind of like you."

You splashed some water around. "Okay. I love you."

I pushed some bubbles around. "Okay."

And that is why, dear, sweet Susie, I can never forgive myself. I'm sorry—so, *so* sorry. I can never say it enough, because on that clear morning in April, I committed the greatest sin of all.

We were going to the library to study together, then out for lunch, then manicures, then a movie. It was going to be our day. I was seventeen, due to graduate from high school the next month, and you had agreed eagerly to this sisters' outing. We had been friends for eight years, since you became my weed-pulling helper at three, and even though the age difference was significant, I think I loved you more than the rest of your admirers, because you weren't just my little sister—you were my friend.

"I think you should get a haircut too, while we're out," you said.

"Why?"

"Something short and sassy. To transition you from high school to college."

I laughed. "I don't think a haircut is going to make much of a difference."

"No, it will. If the layers are done properly they'll frame your face beautifully and you will appear much older, which will be great for all those college parties."

You were eleven and loved the beauty tips in the teen magazines I brought home every now and then. I usually ignored them, because they all sounded the same and rarely had anything interesting to say, but you devoured them, and always informed me if there was something you thought I needed to know.

"I don't think I'll be going to many parties," I told you dryly, but you just shook your head.

"Nope, sorry, you're wrong. You'll be so popular it will make all the sorority girls sick with envy. And you'll have a different date every weekend."

"Right," I said. "Because I've had so many of those in high school."

"The boys here are losers," you said with a disdainful little sniff. "In college, they will appreciate you."

I doubted it, but you seemed to have your heart set on it. "All right," I agreed. "I'll cut my hair." I glanced over at you. "If you want."

"I do," you said, with a decisive nod. There was a pause. I was thinking about leaving home, thinking about how much was going to change.

"Should I cut my hair?"

I looked over at you. Your soft, brown hair hung in waves on your shoulders, but it had always been manageable at any length.

"I think you'll look great no matter how your hair is cut."

You beamed at me, and I turned down the radio so I could focus on you more easily. The traffic was unusually heavy for this time of morning, especially en route to the library, of all places.

I grinned. "Hey… you want to get matching haircuts?"

"Yes!" Your smile turned a little sheepish. "If you don't think it's too cheesy."

I shook my head. "Nope. I think it'll be great. And it'll make me feel closer to you when I leave." I paused. "I'm really going to miss you, Suz."

"Me too, Marta," you said softly.

Without taking my eyes from the road, I reached over and took your hand. It was slender and pale, just like mine, and I thought of all the piano duets we had played together since you'd started your lessons.

You knew was I was thinking, and squeezed my hand. "We can play duets over the phone, right?"

My eyes filled. "Yeah, of course," I said. "Of course we will."

You sighed and leaned against the window without letting go of my hand. "Okay." There was another pause, and I had just managed to get a hold on my emotions when you said, "I love you."

I looked over at you. "I love you too," I said.

I didn't see it. Neither of us did—that huge, silver truck barreling out of nowhere.

Maybe that's not true. I did see it, but only for a millisecond before it hit the side of the car. It smashed into the window where you were resting your head, and the glass shattered and the car dented in so far it nearly folded in half and we went spinning across the pavement, ricocheting off other cars before we rolled—once, twice, three times—into the ditch.

I screamed and screamed and shut my eyes, but those moments when we were upside down seemed to stretch into eternity. We landed upright. I couldn't hear anything. I was dizzy and my arm had been so thoroughly crushed that I was certain it couldn't be saved. They were going to amputate my arm, and I'd be a freak. Forget the haircut, what I needed was a prosthetic arm.

"Susie…" I moaned.

You didn't answer. I opened my eyes, managing to turn my head, just enough to look at you, then wished I hadn't.

I stared at you, even though it wasn't really you anymore. You were gone, and only your body—your perfect hair and your beautiful eyes and your charming smile—was left behind. I didn't see the blood, didn't see the horrible thing that had happened to you. I just saw the empty shell that was once my little sister, and I couldn't breathe.

When they pulled me out of the car they had to pry my hand from yours; we had still been holding hands when the truck hit. My arm, two ribs, and my shoulder were broken, but the most painful part of my removal from the car was when they peeled our fingers apart. I started crying then, and calling your name. Susie, sweetheart, wake up. Please, Susie, say something. Susie, Susie, please, *please* don't go.

They laid me on the stretcher and I stared up into the sky. I looked straight into the sun without blinking, and it burned circles inside my eyes. My hair tickled my nose as the soft, spring breeze brushed it across my face. We had landed in an azalea bush planted near the street, and the fuchsia flowers were scattered across the ground.

A battered azalea somehow found its way onto my stomach, and I cried harder as I watched it sway when they lifted me up into the ambulance.

After your funeral, I knelt down in front of your grave.

As the dew seeped into my black skirt, I carefully laid a lock of my dark hair onto your grave, beside a pair of fuchsia azaleas—one large, one small— and a weed I'd pulled from your favorite azalea bush in our backyard.

It rained the morning you were born, but Susie—sweet, beautiful, baby sister—the morning you died, the weather was perfect.

GENERATIONS
Rowan F.

17 (F) of Kent, England

Far back,

Seeds rouse and

Stretch

Into the hard limbs of generations.

His hand on the page tracing

The sown and unsown,

The branches and the roots

Of his legacy.

One line longer than the others,

As the tree awoke,

Broke the Earth's clay

And spilt the seeds of the next generation across the paper.

Other places old stumps,

Hidden from the stirring sunbeams

Asleep

Waiting for the morning

(that will never come)

When the blood line of ink might attach and name.

A date, to spread across the field

And make that place a home.

Waiting for the morning when the old stump wakes

To find it has grown gently into another's side.

To touch, to warm, to whisper.

EVERGREEN
Kylan R.

18 (M) of Oregon, USA

– goddess,

we can hear you.–

Running as fast a she can, branches scratching at her naked arms and raw pink cheeks. Her breath is so heavy in her lungs and her legs churn up and down like engineparts. Trees lean in at her, creating hallways, waiting there with the expectant faces of relatives around a deathbed. The wind is trying to gut her. Open her up and spill out all her organs, peel out her bones until she is tender and jellied. She has to find him. She just has to. Where has he gone?

Her heart throbs like a hot day.

They walked through the long grass, all shook up by the wind, threshing around them with wild, contemptible movements. She insisted on holding his hand, because she was afraid that he might disappear and then she would be left all alone with Father and his gin-breath. Her hand was sweaty and warm and he could hear her grinding her teeth like the tumblers of a deadbolt lock. Her chin jutted forward and her eyes were cupped towards the woods. Gil could feel the vibrations of her anger and her need, rising through her skin.

She was afraid that he'd blow away in the wind, like a kiss.

They stepped around the boggy creek that ran through the field before the woods and walked onto the dirt road, scarred with potholes and etched with tiretracks. Dry weeds grew up along the side of the road and they kicked up dust as they walked on it, clotting the air with redness.

Gil understood his sister's need. And he cared about her enough to support her, to sit by her side on these days at the base of a tree. She was pretty much all the family he had anyway, and there were only a couple more years until she could move out. It was her method of release, coming to these woods. This was how she kept from blowing up and killing Father in his sleep with a kitchen knife.

She stopped and bent down to tie her shoe and Gil kicked over a rock with grubs wriggling underneath it like loose teeth. Smiling, she looked up at him. Her smile was genuine and it reminded him of mom's smile, toothy and lipless, full of grace and old time religion. She smiled at him so pure and happy that he felt a little bit guilty for having the pack of Virginia Slims in his back pocket to smoke while she was asleep. He'd stay close by, though. He had to have something to do. She wouldn't understand that. She wouldn't understand that bumming around in the woods wasn't his idea of a good time.

She got up and took him by the hand again and they crossed over the low place in the barbed wire fence and into the woods.

–goddess,

we hear your deadbreath in the nighttime. we touch you with our thinkthoughts and our pictures in the dark are put into your head. shuck this weakness! why do you cling to these flaws? it is hard. we know this. it is hard to take away the stinkrot and the easy marrow of fingertips and hopelessness, because you know no better. we have seen it. played over and over and over again across the silverkissed sky. we have seen as these little spirits of yours are ground up, smashed under heels, and they tickle our thinkthoughts more than maybe you would expect.

but we know you.

we know the touchfeel of your heaviness.

bloom. if you bloom. if you bloom.

the stars are easily accessible, easily stolen by us. –

We come here and sit by the creek and listen as it speaks to us, preaches to us, when Father is home. His face gets so ugly sometimes, and his words get so hard. His eyes get all red-veined and cracked, like the land during a drought, and his tongue works and his fingers grope at the air as he shudders towards us, big and angry. He touches that bottle above the cupboards and he turns into a stranger, I swear. We don't know him much anymore. He's as firey as the good book on his insides.

He's made of nothing more than old, used up promises and sloshing with gin when he walks.

He sloshes with tears, too, sometimes. But we know him even less when he does.

The hush of the woods crawls over us like the tide, and we let it. Gil and I, we just sit there and close our eyes and tilt our heads back and I run my fingers through his hair, the strands knotted and tangled. I feel him get bored and excitable under me sometimes, but I just loosen up even further and let myself bend and creak and jive with the trees in the wind and he gets my drift and bends along with me.

I feel real good here, in these woods.

But I also feel a little out of place, too. I feel like a sinner in a church. All the trees with their spindly, ribbed fingers and their bark as rough and ancient and full of stories as grandma's skin and the creek making quiet music. The dirt moves beneath me and everything seems to be working, working, working, toiling as quietly and industriously as ants in a candyjar. Here, I feel the real stickiness of life. I get it stuck in my hair and between my toes. Things are soft and alive. There is so much virginity here, even though a road runs no more than a mile away from it and kids play music up real loud when they pass by, unmindful and irreverent.

I guess I feel foreign.

I guess I feel stained, you know?

Gil has such cold, brown skin.

I run my fingers down it and sink away into sleep.

Her eyes scuttle around in her sockets and they are red. Her ears buzz with fruitflies of worry and despair and terror and when she blinks everything before her kind of jumps and slides, shadowy and spidery against the sky. Her jaw is clenched as she turns around and around, searching.

She calls his name repeatedly until it runs off her tongue without her even thinking about it, until her voice gets all scratchy, like a handful of nails. She prays, prays, prays as she turns. Please, Lord God, please don't let him be gone. I wouldn't be able to stand it. I wouldn't be able to live.

There's this feeling in her stomach.

She's knows he's gone from her. She knows.

– goddess,

take comfort.

there is no greater gift than the gift of foreverness, a concept hard for you, we know. think of it like a string that you unravel every day of your life until your breath stops in your throat and your heart shrivels up like a prune but you keep going, not feeling, not feeling. your fingers keep pulling the string, but everything has stopped around you and you know that there is no rest and you embrace the idea. because it is comforting to you that there is no end. there is no daylight or moonlight or cold or hot or any laughing or any crying because you chose not to let it matter to you anymore.

it is a highfeeling. we do not expect you to know. but we know.

take comfort. –

I wake up with a dead taste in my mouth and eyelids like creaky cellar doors. I lick my lips and I just sit there and listen for a little bit, listen more to the creek and the nymphsong of the wind whittling at the branches of the big sugarpine trees.

"Sure is nice out today, huh, Gil?" I say and I reach up to stroke his hair but he's not laying across my lap no more. I open my eyes. I see that he's gone and I call his name, which echoes and dangles from the braches of trees like hangmen. I call again, but there's nothing.

The trees draw in closer, begging with their bony hands. I stand up and that polished arrowhead that Gil found in Mr. Thompson's cowfield and carries around with him like some kind of goodluck charm falls out of my skirts and into the dirt. I stand there and stare at it, not daring to touch it. The silence presses its body up real close to mine, electric as flesh on flesh, and whispers in my ears to stay, to stay.

But I start running.

I run as fast as I can into the woods, calling his name.

– goddess,

you are distressed over the smallest of things. –

She can hear his voice. She can hear it faint and airy, like a prayer. Sobbing and frantic, she follows it, strung along. It weaves through the trees as soundlessly as an Indian and it sounds trapped and hurried. Her skirts are muddy. Her face is hot and pink as the slobbertongue of a dog.

"Gil!"

GilGilGilGil.

The trees snatch the name up and keep it in their cobweb souls. She's not so sure about these woods anymore. They twist in front of her. She falls among the trees and tears herself away from them and she imagines a darkness welling up behind them, inside of them, blossoming with black sunflower faces.

– goddess – they whisper.

– bloom with us –

Gil's voice is very loud now. She can hear it clearly. It invades her ears and burrows holes into her thoughts until they lose their form and break apart. She falls to her knees.

Flora! Flora, I'm here, I'm here!

"Where!" she screams, clutching her ears.

I'm right here. Right here! Look up!

She looks up.

A tree stands slenderbodied and wise in front of her.

– letting go, unpeeling your inhibitions, is hard. we know. but we see something different in you. we see a new kind of light, something that only comes along so often. it is a hard and tired life you lead. but here is rest. we are rest. inside of us, there is a warmth and a sereneness.

goddess,

we know.

you can know, too. –

I can't believe what I'm hearing. But it feels right and good. I realize now. I know now. I touch the treebark in front of me and it is hot and real and squirming inside like a baby. Bloom, it tells me, with Gil's voice. I feel my toes wriggling into shoots, I can feel it, and my true fingers cracking out of my skin as seedling roots. The sun, it is so drunken, and a purple moistness creeps up through my veins. Dreams scatter around my vision like pollen and I can feel Gil at my side again, churning and alive and I can feel this strange new world tugging at my clothing, undressing me of it and I let it. I give in to this dusklight seduction, nervous as a newlywed, as a virgin. bloom, it tells me.

the soil is sweet. i run my slippery toes through it, scrunching through it. i feel at peace. i feel the stopping of my breath, the corking of my weakness, and i lift my arms stiff and heavy and old. we see so much. we see the body below us, nothing to it now. fragile and susceptible to the wind as trash. let it blow away. we let it blow away.

Gil followed her footprints, mushed and heavy in the soil, for at least a mile. He called her name, but it went unanswered. He had to catch his breath once and he leaned up against the base of a tree, wondering if she went back home. He had only been away for a minute or two for a smoke, and he knew how much she loved this place and he knew how tired she had felt under him.

He walked for another fifteen minutes.

Right as he was about to turn back, he found Flora's naked body under a sugarpine tree, curled up and whiteskinned as a tapeworm, with her fingers deep in the soil and dirt stuffed in her mouth and peace on her face.